October,
Eight O'Clock

ALSO BY NORMAN MANEA
On Clowns: The Dictator and the Artist

October,
Eight O'Clock

NORMAN MANEA

TRANSLATED BY

Cornelia Golna, Anselm Hollo,
Mara Soceanu Vamos, Max Bleyleben, and
Marguerite Dorian and Elliott B. Urdang

GROVE PRESS
New York

The stories in this collection have been translated by Cornelia Golna, with the following exceptions: "The Balls of Faded Yarn," "Weddings," and "The Partition" by Mara Soceanu Vamos; "Tale of the Enchanted Pig" by Marguerite Dorian and Elliott B. Urdang; "Summer" by Max Bleyleben; "The Turning Point" by Anselm Hollo.

Grove Press
841 Broadway
New York, NY 10003

Published in Canada by General Publishing Company, Inc.

"The Sweater" originally appeared in a different form in *TriQuarterly*.

Library of Congress Cataloging-in-Publication Data
Manea, Norman.
     [Short stories. English. Selections]
     October, eight o'clock / Norman Manea ; translated by Cornelia
Golna . . . [et al.]. — 1st ed.
     Translated from the Romanian.
     1. Manea, Norman—Translations into English. I. Title.
     II. Title: October, 8 o'clock.
     PC840.23.A47A26   1992
     859'.334—dc20   91-36377

     ISBN 0-8021-3371-1 (pbk.)

Manufactured in the United States of America

Designed by Irving Perkins Associates

First English-language Edition 1992

10 9 8 7 6 5 4 3 2 1

CONTENTS

October,
Eight O'Clock

THE SWEATER

SHE WOULD leave every Monday and return every Friday. Each time in tears, as though she were saying good-bye for the last time. Next week she might not find the strength to go—so much could happen in a week. A miracle, and she wouldn't need to leave, to be separated from us. The sky might suddenly open and we might find ourselves in a real train, not like the cattle cars they had unloaded us from in this emptiness at the end of the world. It would be a warm, brightly lit train with soft seats . . . kind, gentle ladies would serve us our favorite foods, as befits travelers returning from the other world. Or, perhaps, even before Friday, the day she was due back, this endless ashen sky would come crashing down to swallow us or redeem us, this sky that we awaited to enter once and for all, so that everything might come to an end.

We waited by the window to see her appear like a phantom out of the smoky steppes. She looked like a shadow, withered and gloomy. She walked hurriedly, panting, bent under the weight of her sack, which bulged with the days and nights of her labor. Father's work earned him a quarter loaf of bread a day. If it hadn't been for her, we would have faded very rapidly, right at the beginning. She had insisted on working, she had pleaded, he knew, until finally they gave her permission to go to the villages in the vicinity. How could she have escaped?

They had let her go, accepting her pleas with cynical good-will—a game worth playing, if only so they could interrupt it suddenly with greater cruelty.

Monday to Friday she knitted for peasants whose language she did not understand. We knew very well that at any moment it could all come to an end right here in the barracks where she left us, or in the heated houses where she worked, mutely, for some potatoes, a handful of beans or flour, sometimes even for some cheese, prunes, or apples. Only she still believed that we would survive if we held fast to anything that might save us.

Friday, then, was a kind of new beginning, as if we had won yet another reprieve. She staggered toward us, weighed down, dragging, bent under the sack. The joy of the reunion was so intense that none of us could speak. She was agitated, like a madwoman, as if she could not believe that she was seeing us again. She fluttered helpless and alarmed from one wall to the other, without coming near us. Later, with difficulty, she composed herself, gathering enough strength to open the sack she had thrown down on entering the room. Once she bent over to divide up the contents, it meant that she had calmed down.

As was her habit, she reached into the sack and set on the floor six piles, one for each of the following six days: potatoes, beets. She put aside three apples. No one expected anything but the usual. She had raised her hand to her forehead before huddling, exhausted, on the floor. "I've brought something else, too." This did not necessarily mean a surprise. We were not expecting anything different: we had forgotten how to wish for other gifts; we were amazed that she was able to do even this much.

With difficulty, she pulled out something from the bottom of the sack, as if she were lifting it, exhausted, by its ears or its big front paws. She didn't have the strength to hold it in her arms and show it to us. She let it fall from her skeletal hands onto the gaping opening of the bag. There it looked even thicker, heavier.

It could only be for Father, of course, but it was too beautiful—or perhaps for that very reason, because anyone who saw it would have wanted it for himself, even if it was meant for someone else. It sparkled with colors, as if the magician who would save us wanted to demonstrate to us what he could do. The night enveloped us in smoke, cold, and darkness; we heard nothing but explosions, screams, the barks of the guards, crows, and frogs. We had long ago forgotten such glitter.

She had not had the chance to unfold it so that we could see it whole, but that did not matter: clearly it was real. Even our rescue now seemed closer, or at least possible, since we had been granted the sight and touch of such a miracle.

Unable to resist, I moved closer to stroke it. It looked soft, supple; you could wrap yourself in it and have no care in the world. My hand caressed the sleeves and the neck. I squeezed it, kneaded it, turned it this way and that. I laid it down and opened it up; then I folded it back together to take to Father. I would have remained motionless, transfixed, if only she had opened her mouth at that moment to tell me what I was waiting to hear, that it was in fact for me.

But it would have tempted anyone, and he deserved it more than anybody else, since he had lost all hope long ago.

It was thick; it looked big; without a doubt it had been made for him. I had to give it to him; it was pointless to wait.

"No, it's not for Father," she managed to whisper, as if she were guilty of something.

I stopped, bewildered, holding it in my arms, blinded by its colors and warmth. I realized that I should have kept out of it, or at least have known how things stood from the very beginning.

At last the poor woman had made something for herself. On the snow-covered roads of the steppe she would have more use for it than we. I should have thought of it immediately; I should have reminded myself of how she looked when she left— wrapped only in sackcloth, her feet swathed in rags. Such blindness, such stupidity, was inexcusable. I almost wept with mortification. I did not want to let go, it looked so soft and supple, but it was hers, I no longer had anything to say. I unfolded it to look at it one more time. Now it did not look so big. She had made it for herself; for once she had thought about what she needed.

I turned and went toward the corner of the room that seemed warmest, where the good fairy was huddled.

"The sweater is for Mara," she said.

It had gotten dark, and I could no longer see her. I could not tell if she had smiled at me as I had thought, or whether she had collapsed, as sometimes happened. A purple, glacial haze descended over and around me.

I couldn't help myself: I remained immobile for a long time, my head buried in the softness of the front and of the sleeves; I had nestled in so as to never leave. But I soon sensed, through the welcoming thickness of the wool, the glacial silence, ever heavier, becoming unbearable; I could not even hear them breathe.

I turned around and walked resolutely toward Mara, and deposited it in the girl's arms.

I looked at it more carefully the next day. It did not seem so extraordinary. First, it had been knitted only out of knots, you could see that. I turned it inside out, I showed it to Mara, to convince her: one knot after another, as though it had grown out of leftover bits of yarn. And the color—it is true that in certain parts it had more red, but otherwise it was a confusing mishmash; you couldn't make anything out of it. White with gray, black, a trace of yellow, a remnant of green and another, darker green; a gray stripe, a bit of rotten-earth brown next to a purple plum; over there a tip of pink ham, next to it a bird's red-and-yellow beak. Of course, it had not been knitted for a girl; anybody could see that. But I did not tell her. Mara's position was special, they said, and had to remain so at all costs.

We loved her excessively, we looked after her more vigorously than we did ourselves—that is what they always urged us to do. I could not point out to her that it was too big for her, that it had a boy's crew neck. She could have seen that for herself, after all—she was old enough—but to do that she would have had to take it off occasionally and look at it. They allowed her everything, of course. Since she had asked to keep it on, they let her. She even slept in it, completely dressed, at least for the first few days. It's true that the cold was biting both day and night, especially at night. But if you tried to put on more layers, the same plague befell you every time: lice. Undress and wash yourself, put on other rags, clean ones; we boil them and check all the seams; otherwise it's a disaster. I knew very well that they would never have tolerated me sleeping with the same clothes on three nights in a row. But they let her, even though she was the one they protected most determinedly. The moment they heard that someone had fallen ill at the other end of the barracks, they would start examining her; obsessed, they would feel her forehead, her neck, they would look into her eyes, at her hair, her nails. What panic if by any chance she should have a hot forehead or warm hands. . . .

She must return alive at all costs, they would repeat in a whisper every time. She had ended up among us by mistake. What would they say if she of all people was lost and we returned? That we had only looked after our own skins? Perhaps her mother knew where we were and was on her way here, documents in hand, to establish the truth. The little girl had nothing to do with the curse on us; she was innocent. She had been sent to stay with an old family friend for a few weeks, far away from the hospital where her mother had been admitted. Caught in the catastrophe, mixed up with us and taken away, she had been brought as far as this. Protests convinced no one. They did not have time for clarifications; we were not believed. Of course, we too, in our own way, were innocent; to keep hope alive, everyone shouted that. But the case of this guest of ours seemed much more serious to us all. If the situation was not cleared up and the poor thing was detained with us for the duration, she must, in any case—on this everybody agreed—be the last, she must survive everybody. They whispered in corners when the little girl could not hear them; they vied with one another over who would take care of her; they did not know what to do to make her happy, how to keep her from harm. I should have guessed that the gift could only be for her, that they would let her do with it as she pleased.

Only now, on the fourth day, could I look at it calmly. A miracle, I could no longer deny it. I might have asked to borrow it for one night at least. She would have let me; she would even have given it to me, if I had asked her. She was always kind to me. But it was not allowed, I knew, though I could admire it without embarrassment for hours on end. Not even the cleverest magician would have been capable of something more wonderful. The knots made it stronger, concentrating and increasing the warmth underneath while allowing it to look light and smooth on the surface. As for the colors—strange islands of dye, now black, now green, now blue—one could run and dip one's fingers and eyes as one pleased, until one came across a patch as red as African sand, an ashen tip of a cloud touched by a golden ray, the sun, flowers. A whole day would not have been enough to explore all those constantly, dizzyingly evolving continents. I did not have time to become bored with it, nor to borrow it or wear it to the point of indifference.

The following week, Mara's cheeks were red with fever. She ended up abandoning it, leaving it alone in the corner by the window. I looked at it; I thought about it, but I did not touch it, although I longed to.

Mara got worse; she was dying. Since my grandparents' illness, I knew how it began and how it would end. She would die soon; they would not be able to help her. I knew that the hours when she revived, happy and talkative once more, were deceptive.

She would have had no reason, then, not to give it to me. The disease would progress. The days had become longer, they seemed endless; death was drawing near, I felt it. Frightened, I waited to see the beloved little girl suddenly stiffen. Perhaps if she offered it to me now . . . a vindication that could alter the course of events. They would not have hesitated to give it to me if that gesture could have saved her—but it wasn't my fault, I was not responsible for her illness, and anyway they weren't able to find medicines for her.

I did not participate in their arrangements or in their sobs when it came time to bury her, together with all her things, beside my grandparents, at the edge of the forest. I waited, feverishly, still hoping they would forget. But Mother snatched it out of the corner and threw it savagely on top, over the other things.

They stood near the little girl a few more moments, sobbing, choking, holding one another close. Although she wasn't a member of our family, Mara was the first to follow my grandparents. She had become one of us. When they were ready to carry the coffin out of the house, Father reached over with his big hand, felt around, found it, pulled it to one side, and let it fall behind him. Mother saw; she looked at him for a long time, but said nothing: she accepted that it be saved.

We returned from the forest late and shivering. It was raining, and the mud stuck to our rags. Wet clods of earth had covered Mara. Since the departure of my grandparents, I knew that she also would not return. I remembered how she used to huddle up against the cold with her arms around my neck. We adored her sudden, full laugh. Silent, we stretched out on the muddy earthen floor, where night surprised us.

I did not go near it, I did not touch it. I only stole a few glances at it where it lay abandoned, gloomy, lifeless. Nor did anyone tell me to take it the next day, although the room seemed to have become even colder and damper. Monday, Mother left again; that afternoon, when we had finished working, Father put it on my shoulders. I felt the sleeves slide over my chest; I pulled them on and put my head through its warmth. It fit snugly, as if it had been made especially for me. I would have gone out in the yard to show myself or would have walked proudly around the room at least, but I did not dare. I crouched; at last I had what I had wanted for so many days. I was shaking, I could no longer control myself.

My joy, however, was short-lived. The very next day I felt the sleeves hang limp on my shoulders. This was the signal, I remembered. It had started the same way with my grandparents and then with Mara. The sickness was prowling nearby; it crept in slowly, unnoticed, seeping in little by little, only to break out suddenly toward evening when those who were attacked shook, dizzy with fever, then collapsed, unable to say even a word.

The commotion would start: asking the neighbors for medicine, an aspirin at least, or a little alcohol. In the end the thermometer appeared. It was the only one in the entire camp, kept by an old madwoman in a piece of dirty blanket. The thermometer was hard to obtain; you had to insist anxiously. It was passed cautiously from hand to hand, like a talisman, until it reached the sickbed. We all feared that it would break, and thus our last contact with a normal universe, to which we still pretended to belong, would disappear.

Then the doctor would appear. And so it was this time too, but in place of the distinguished gentleman with slender glasses, confident in his ministration, a tired, ragged, hunched-over consumptive had come. We called him "doctor" too; he also had small white hands, which he no longer washed at the beginning and end of each visit, as he had in the past. Gestures and consultations had been reduced to a minimum.

He had laid his hand on the little girl's forehead, he had looked at her fingers; then he had felt for her pulse, counting the beats with his lips. He had uncovered her thin, yellowish body, turned it to this side and that, and pointed to the spots, one here, one there: the disease had taken complete possession of the little body. There was nothing else to do but raise his hands and mutter the name of the affliction, which would last only a few more days. Only a miracle, only a miracle. . . . He raised his hands once more, resignedly, to pray, as did every-one, for the miracle; then he slipped out, bent and ashamed, just as he had come.

Dusk was descending; I felt the light grow more and more tired, but more than that I felt the bitter cold that suddenly pierced me. The evening chill had begun to settle in when I felt something strange, as if I had been abandoned, as if it no longer protected me; inert and cold, it now hung lifeless on my shoulders. It must have been carrying the disease the whole time. It had betrayed Mara too, but she had not succeeded in taking it with her when she died. Now it was my turn. I would have torn it off me, burned it, thrown it far away. But it was too late; none of that would do any good.

I didn't want to end in that dark, damp grave where one did not know what to expect. It was my fault, I knew it. I should not have agonized so impatiently for those colors and their warmth. If I had controlled myself, if I had waited; if I had not spied so shamelessly on Mara's suffering and what had followed, until it covered me . . . I should not have been so weak and oblivious, so impatient that when it came into my possession I was overcome by tears of joy. My baseness and greed must have been seen, been noticed. Had I given it up, if not at the beginning, at least after Mara's death, the punishment might have been avoided.

I could not stand it any longer; I went to the window. Father, as usual, was looking through the narrow aperture of light for a miracle or a disaster. Toward evening, hopelessness overcame him; he no longer knew how to suppress it.

"The disease. The disease, I feel sick." At first he did not hear me. He turned abruptly, he placed his hand on my brow, then on my neck. He dragged me to the window and asked me to count, to stick out my tongue, to open my eyes. "You're pale, very pale, but there is nothing wrong with you," he said, and picked me up in his big arms so that I would go to sleep.

I did not have the strength to speak. I pointed a few times to the infected sleeves. I placed my fingers over the diseased collar, but he did not notice. The deep of the night had already fallen; he covered me with his large smile, he bent over me, his palm on my moist forehead.

I woke up in the coffin, being lowered into the grave next to Mara; then there was nothing. I was shivering; day had come; I wanted to tell them that I would not make it to Friday, so there would be no one to save me. But she came that night. I couldn't see anything, only a thick cloud, ever thicker, and I heard her frightened voice above me.

I felt—on my neck, in my ear—the sound of anxious breathing. "Thank God I've come back, I've come back in time," she was saying. I also heard the thin voice of the doctor gasping nearby. "He doesn't have spots; there are no symptoms." That is what he said: "symptoms." It sounded nice, "symptoms." I dragged the word after me, I was falling, plunging; symptoms, it was almost reassuring, I was sliding, going down; I no longer knew anything. Wet slippery fish brushed my burning lips; they licked my ears, and I floated with them. Now and then I shook the waves from my chest and tried to open my eyes. I saw Mara, opaque, made of wax; the sharp yellow teeth of the doctor, and again the grave.

The drowning probably lasted several days, then finally I heard once more that familiar voice: "I feel better about leaving; I'm glad it's over." I had escaped the arms of death; coming to, I staggered as I attempted my first steps along the walls, with Father's arm to support me, to the window facing the steppe that had swallowed everything.

I managed to ask if I still had spots.

"You never had them. It wasn't the illness. Only a scare, that's what the doctor said. You were delirious, raving the whole time. 'It's stuck to me,' you kept saying. 'It's stuck to me,' and you tried to raise your hands."

He lifted me under my arms so I could look out the window. He gave me hot gruel. On Friday morning the steppe gave Mother back to us. "I came earlier; I told them you were sick. They gave me some lard to give you strength."

And so I gained strength. I could look at it again. Defeated, diminished, subdued in a corner, ready to serve me. But I had changed. I left it alone; I no longer looked at it. They had covered me with a thick blanket; I no longer felt even a hint of cold. Everyone was around me, determined not to abandon me.

It had shrunk, become smaller. In the end I allowed it to win me over. It hadn't proved dangerous. In the time it had lain rolled up next to the damp walls, its prickly, uneven hairs had

softened somewhat. I put my nose, my whole face, in its rough-
ness, once so soft and good, to let myself be intoxicated by its
warmth, like that of toasted bread or boiled potatoes, or by the
smell of fresh sawdust, or the fragrance of milk, of rain, of
leaves, or by the longing for pencils and apples. But it was not
like that; rather a strange odor, that of mold. Something rotten
and penetrating. Or only sharp, suffocating, I don't remember.
It had become darker, and unfamiliar, unappealing.

In the next few days we grew more used to each other; we
were starting to know each other again. We were slowly finding
each other; it was becoming its old self, more and more fluffy
and warm. The colors had revived; a world of dyes. Still, its
nearness frightened me, oppressed me. I had wanted it to be
mine alone. My impatience had hastened Mara's death! I shud-
dered, although no one else had found me out. I approached
it without courage, weak. My arms would get tangled in it; I
could not get it over my head. When at last it clung to me,
already too tight, it seemed to choke me. I was no longer afraid
of the sickness. Mara had taken away its power, I knew it, it
couldn't pass on the disease. Only the feeling of guilt, the fear,
the embrace of the boiling-hot sleeves that clung to my neck
just as the little girl tried to huddle next to me every night
against the cold.

But I was getting used to it, and it had also calmed down. It
no longer jumped to my eyes, to remind me. It obeyed me; it
served me, ever less portentous, acquiescent. Often I forgot my
obsessions; I had acquired a certain confidence.

But I did not wear it to the doctor's burial; that would have
been too much. It was during a terrible snowstorm, and I shook
with fear and bitter cold. I had hidden it well so no one would
find it. I forgot about it for quite a few days and set it free only
much later, when the burials had multiplied to several every
day. There was no reprieve anywhere, there was no avoiding

it. They died by the dozens; the curse fell at random, precisely
on those who least expected it. They no longer had time for me,
nor I for myself; the terror had become universal, beyond
measure, had swallowed us all. We were shrinking, dazed,
oblivious of ourselves and of everyone else.

Nothing counted anymore, neither grief nor shame. It had
understood that too. Its colors and smell faded and didn't
attract attention any longer. It was merely functional. I wore it
every day—it protected me from the cold, that's all. It fit
perfectly, like a sheath; there was nothing reminiscent of our
previous glorious intimacy. We took no notice of each other, we
defended ourselves as best we could, though we were defenseless. The winds off the steppes kept drawing nearer to take their
pick. Their voracious howling drowned out all fear. It would
not have been possible to hear a sad, choked sob, guilty and
shameful.

Each day stalked us. We forgot the days; we waited, listening
for the maddening fury of the night. The time we lived in
pursued us; there was nothing to be done. Time itself had
sickened, and we belonged to it.

DEATH

THE GAME required that the little girls freeze when the sound hit them. Not a muscle would twitch. They did not blink, they did not move, not even when a shout or a stone, hurled against the fence to simulate a rifle shot, or a shard of glass shattering against the wall, caught them in full flight, or jumping, carrying water, combing their hair, or in the strangest of positions, unable to hold their balance for very long.

And it had happened, not too long before, that two of them were caught perched on a window ledge, about to fall. The window was almost a full story off the ground. Their thin legs could no longer hold, in a few moments they would fall backward. Luckily a hulking fellow who was just passing by managed to catch them in time.

Sometimes, as the rules required, they remained still for up to an hour in the position in which the signal caught them. Hands raised, leg in the air, neck twisted or back bent. Arms almost brushing the ground, stiffened in the act of picking up the lining of the sleeve of an old coat, or even, unbelievably, the still-greasy waxed-paper wrapping of a lump of butter that had somehow made its way from the guards' canteen. The desire, no matter how strong, to complete the movement did not prevail. They were dead—no temptation could have awakened them.

The little girls had invented "playing mannequin." They tried to become instant ladies. The motionlessness of these little statues, soiled and ragged, simulated the elegance of a world that they imagined still retained an ideal of refinement and grace. Yet the game could have had another name. The way they froze, almost naked, skeletal, their motionlessness, the way they stopped suddenly and no longer moved at all, holding their breath, presaged something sinister.

As he watched them, the boy had more than once asked himself whether their game did not attract, even hasten, such evil. He seemed to feel the presence of the barrel of a hidden gun taking aim, nearby, behind a wall or from a watch tower. . . . The guards would have been tremendously amused by that game. In the moment the children got the signal, the shout that imitated a rifle shot, they could not know that one of them had been gunned down. They could not take in that the rifle shot was real: the fall of the target was not part of the game.

They were proud of the skill they had acquired to seize, in their motionlessness, the haughtiness and the glamour of another world where, they imagined, or perhaps had been told by their elders, such ladies and gentlemen still existed, made to be admired from a distance, from behind glass. The boy thought he could see the muzzle of the gun or the smaller muzzle of a revolver hidden a few steps away, stalking them, suddenly giving the signal for a different game, a game that would have amused the soldiers terribly.

The day when the two little girls were caught by the sound on the window ledge—near the roof of the dormitory stacked with beds—and were about to lose their balance but were saved in the nick of time by Lică, the gigantic cousin with curly red hair, now also tinged with white, the boy was sure that this time disaster had struck. Petrified, he did not open his eyes for several seconds: the two brunettes were running again. They appeared frightened, it is true; but they were, incredible as it may seem, alive and jolly.

All around, on the other side of the fence, flowers were blooming. Spring had come, you could hear birds. He had no way of recognizing them, he could not name them, no one had found the time to talk to him about flowers and birds, nor about the many insects that had come out with the sun.

He was leaning against one of the fence posts. His eyes closed, he was abandoning himself to the laziness that was growing inside him. He felt very hot, and unbuttoned his shirt down to his waist. It was a very colorful shirt made of remnants of cloth sewn together at random; Mother had gotten hold of them who knows where. He had undone the two buttons, a pink one from an eiderdown blanket at the neck, and the other, sewn on low at the waist, big and black, from an overcoat, as Lică kept repeating to make fun of him. He opened the shirt to uncover his thin, bony, and yellowish chest. He stayed there, his eyes closed, the lids quivering and pulsating with the light.

The sun warmed his slender and as yet unformed ribs, vulnerable to the sting of the bullet about to explode.

He got it right in the chest. The first thought, even before he opened his eyes: "There was no sound, there was no shot." Nothing.

He could hear the buzzing nearby, on his chest. He felt the needle buried deep and the place where it had entered. He thrashed his arms about convulsively, he screamed. This was death, it would not last more than a few moments, everything was collapsing, there was no more time. He ran, pale, stabbed: a dead man with black, frightened eyes; the yellow insect was following him, buzzing around his shoulders. He raised his hands, trying to protect himself, stumbling, rocking backward. He whirled around a few times, the shirt had completely fallen off his shoulders, he turned around, continued to run, without looking back. He jumped, the earth opened under each one of his leaps; he ran with his mouth open, exhausted, sweaty, to catch the final moments, to arrive in time. The pain grew; the poison was rapidly working its way up, he would be too late . . . He hurled himself through the door of the barracks and burst inside.

His uncle was gazing out, as usual, through the boards. The old woman was praying in a corner. They would not be able to help him, they had not even seen him enter. He staggered, soon his strength would ebb, he knew it, he ran next door, then to the neighbors' on the other side, then to others still, down the corridor. He could no longer speak, he was suffocating, his cheeks were burning, sticky with tears.

He ran out, went around the courtyard, sobbing, desperate. Time was passing faster and faster; he went to the other barracks, he found her, at last! He managed to show her the swelling on his chest, where he had been hit. He was gasping, he begged her, quick, quick, everything must be tried, immediately. She could still save him, maybe. He had been shot at, hit, stung, something yellow, poisonous. But the rough hand was stroking his head to calm him down. She always wasted time, Mother, in stupid caresses. And look, he no longer had the strength, he was fading fast, not even she understood the disaster. "It's nothing, a bee, it's nothing." Her calm voice terrified him. Not even she understood, and so . . .

He was about to look up, to scream, when he heard behind him a wild, familiar laugh. It was cousin Lică guffawing. That hulking fellow had become more and more emaciated, now he looked like a miserable wretch, but he still had strength. He seemed to have gathered all of it, that oaf, in that torrent of laughter that came crashing over him.

WE MIGHT HAVE
BEEN FOUR

THE DAYS floated white above us—hot-iron white—and from them sparks shot out to frighten us, to burn us, to scatter us.

The forest was waiting for night to fall; we were alive to the rustle that would protect us on our return.

We watched the bundle turn in the water and allow itself to be carried away. We would escape suspicion and its consequences if they found no feathers, traces of blood, or entrails near our temporary refuge. We did not know that suspicion would collect around us anyway, regardless of evidence, that it would hound us, until we finally understood that we could hold out against its motley and changeable veil.

We watched the bundle circle. We hoped that the fears that wore out our days and nights—fear of people, of lice, of uniforms, of hunger—would prove in the end to be powerless, because we would always be three, even four. We watched the bundle whirl around and drift away. And now there was the forest. The heady, fragrant scent with which, time and again, it tried to call or shelter us—a sad, useless cunning that stalked my moments of loneliness and doubt, a slow cunning of trees, earth, leaves, and passing seasons—was a pointless temptation, because we would survive, united against both the fears that sent their poisons at us and the calm green refuge of the forest. We had only to stay together, confident that not one of us would betray the others.

I had thrown away the bundle wrapped in newspaper: now we could leave. But we stayed, our eyes riveted to the water, not knowing why, riveted for no reason to the water, which we suspected was cold.

I felt Mother smile protectively; she put her hand over his to caress him, and he responded with a smile, not to the caress but to the smile, silently watching the water; at last he decided to release us all.

"All right, we can go. . . ."

This did not seem to be enough; no one moved. We were still distracted, daydreaming, letting the moment pass away unaware, and a hand, not the one that had caressed him, a burning hand, slipped through my hair. I knew—after everything I had not managed to prove earlier, on the bridge—that it would be ridiculous for me to play the man, but I had to be the first to tear myself away. Without freeing myself from the caress that was ruffling my hair, I said to everyone and to the forest:

"Let's go, Finlanda."

The two of us started off, ahead of the others. I was walking in step with Finlanda, aware of her hand playing absently with my hair. They found it odd that I called her by her full name; everyone else called her Fina or Anda. It was a funny name—Finlanda. At first I had been sure that all the children would jeer at her, laugh at her name. Perhaps they were going to, but they didn't; when she appeared they stared at her in awe and then, with sudden seriousness, started looking for something among the stones in the road. I was the only one to play with her full name; as always, I said it clearly, flowingly, with a ring, while she, distracted, mussed my hair.

We had reasons to go back contented; the great adventure, to which we had abandoned ourselves with so much pleasure from the night before to the dawn of the day that was now expiring, had passed with unexpected ease and clarity. But Finlanda's burning hand could not rein in my sadness at not having achieved the triumph I wanted at the bridge. I had planned a gesture that would rise like a red, green, white, and yellow flag, a flag of victory and of future victories; I had sought a controlled, slow movement, I wanted to let go slowly, without haste—scorning the emotion that had dominated us and was dominating us now—to nonchalantly release the compromising bundle, hidden all day and destined for the river. The others deserved the gift of such a gesture, and the forest needed to be warned, and I deserved its spectacular effect, a memory to which I would always return as to a reassuring haven in the hard weeks that were to follow, during which it had to be proved again and again that we three, or even four, were stronger than the dogs, the guards, the uniforms, the hunger, the lice, the bullets, the forest, and the base temptation of the meat of a stolen fowl.

Overwhelmed by the many, hurried pleasures I had experienced in that brief interlude, I showed the strain of that night and of that day. Only a few moments after we had stopped on the flimsy wooden bridge far from the foreign village, I dropped the bundle into the swift, clear water too quickly—spared a prolonged agitation, but shamed by the pettiness of the weakling's haste. . . .

The bundle, wrapped in newspaper, full of feathers, of entrails mixed with blood, had circled in the water only briefly. The others, of course, were thinking only of the golden soup and of the fried chicken we had all eaten in the middle of the night till almost dawn, to prolong the undreamed-of feast that had begun when evening set in. It had been a long celebration: first we had to catch it, kill it, pluck its feathers; only then did we put it to boil; the water's merry bubbling, the miraculous frying in oil, the giddiness caused by these fantastic pleasures; we were overwhelmed, held under the spell of the meat's fragrance almost to the point of oblivion.

Of course, as the bundle began to float away, carried off by the stream that scattered the last traces of the forbidden and hasty banquet, the others thought only about the feast that had ended. They did not suspect that I had planned another, the true celebration, and that I had spoiled it: the act that was to redeem, through a deliberate ritual, the greedy rush of the evening before.

Soothed by the murmur of the water and the draining of the day, we were heading home now, with the evening unsettling the forest and somehow finding an echo in each of them—in them, because I could only think back to the chance I had lost, blundering and agitated, of becoming the master of a legend.

But I could feel that their thoughts were scattered, confused, they groped for them with distracted gestures and allowed themselves to be lulled by the night's rustling embrace. Finlanda too was giving in; the hand previously in my hair, without her even realizing it, was now caressing the air that was bathing our bodies; her flowering, indolent body was abandoned to the waves of fresh, cool, intoxicating pine.

They were walking behind us, just as distracted perhaps. Finlanda started to tease me, and I realized that she thought the frozen silence among us four unnatural. I responded to her jokes as she wanted me to: I laughed uncontrollably, overflowing with cheer.

But I was not able to keep laughing for long, as she expected, because it too seemed unnatural to me. I remembered it often being like this. And I remembered too the matter of Mother's dress, the material that was so hard to find, somehow bought or bartered for by Father, the way he had tendered it to her, happy for her happiness; we had all been wearing rags for two years, and now she could make herself a dress. The way she had looked at him, long, questioningly, as if she understood something that did not please her. She told him that it would not look good on her, she had grown too thin with the war, among these foreigners, but she took it nevertheless, and went to the other side of the hostile village, to where Finlanda lived with her parents, and gave her the fabric. Finlanda made herself a dress in which she seemed to float, to be beyond anyone's reach. And then the evening that she appeared at our house in her new dress: how silence fell and she started to tease me and I laughed.

I had laughed like a fool the night before this one too, after the chicken had been plucked, when Mother sent me to invite her to eat with us. I went to the other side of the village, although there were already enough of us. She had hardly arrived before she began to tease me again, to ruffle my hair with a hand so hot it seemed to have been resting on burning coals.

I thought it strange for me to laugh so hard, like a fool. Now I stifled my laughter and turned to look at them; they were not walking side by side but rather one behind the other. Not seeing the trees or the water, their eyes only on their feet, picking their way along behind us.

I realized that they were not even feeling the seductiveness of the forest or of the night, which was rolling in from above and below and from all sides; it was as if they were not there but were just passing through. I knew that I was laughing like a fool and that Finlanda was stroking my hair distractedly. I freed my tousled hair; she did not notice, lost in the intoxication of the dusk or in other reveries I couldn't understand.

To attract his attention when he came up behind me, I turned my head to look at him. He looked up. He looked straight at me, his eyes blank, the way you look at a blind man, or at someone who you know will never grasp what you are saying even though he is next to you. I took a few more steps with my eyes fixed on his. I longed for something in them, some sign of unease, but I saw nothing.

When I turned forward again, a ribbon of the setting sun flashed vividly through a clearing in the forest. We had come to a halt—Finlanda stopped first—mesmerized by the stern, protective mass of the trees in the last painful glow of the day, which lingered for a moment before darkness fell.

I did not know if they would succumb to the forest's sly call, or if they would resist, or if they would help me resist it and remain with them. I felt lost, petrified, having forgotten the bridge and everything else, and only later did I become aware, as through a hazy dream, that Finlanda had detached herself from me and was moving away quietly, leaving behind her a suspended stillness. Moments of silence and forgetfulness went by before another hazy form distanced itself and left too—I was confused, alone with the sad, heavy burden that weighed on my chest, a burden that I did not want to understand. It frightened me—I did not want it.

I don't know how long I remained with my hand on the rough bark of the tree, looking into the yawning emptiness around me. Long moments passed, as in a fleeting sleep. When I looked up I saw that the order in which we had come had broken down. Finlanda had moved far off, ever more absent. Not too far behind her, he too was moving off, as if caught in the leaves and in the russet light of her flowing hair.

I watched them leave everything behind. I wanted to shout after them, I wanted to hate them, but I liked them, it was always cheerful around them, they always joked with me. . . .

I should have been with her, with Mother, against them. But

she had no patience, she was always sour, anxious. I saw her next to me, with her back turned—she did not know that I had understood, without understanding, the nighttime whispers and arguments not meant for me to hear. She did not see me as she leaned wearily against the tree. Perhaps she alone was caught up in the devouring smells and fragrances of the forest abandoning itself to the night.

I had failed unforgivably at the bridge. Now I was being offered an undeserved chance to redeem myself. I hid behind a tree, determined to make up for the failed surprise that I had planned for her on the bridge. I would remain hidden. She would look for me, sick with worry, and in finding me—much, much later—she would have to give in, drained, to the child-like, tender joy, to the laughter that had so long forgotten her.

I started to shake—it was as though the chicken kept expanding, rising into my throat, my mouth. Sadness over my failure, the vertigo of the forest, my disgust with myself, with them, with the woods, with the food. Overwhelmed with hate, I wanted to burst into a run, to soil the trees and the grass with all the bilious flow that was choking and constricting my mouth, to avenge everything by emptying myself. I was sick in waves, my back against the bark of the tree.

I was shattered, alone; drained of all my strength, I slid down slowly against the rough bark, near the filth that had burst from inside me, the stench of rot and carcass. I was left empty, dizzy, lying on the ground: miles and miles of moments coursed over me until I again heard the leaves, until I felt the grass clutched in my hands. I was coming to, but time seemed never to end; again I became afraid of the bewitching forest, which was preying on my weakness to make me need it, to do with me as it wished. I was not in control of myself; once more I rushed, convinced that she had gone after him and after Finlanda without even a thought for me and for the forest.

Filled with terror, I looked down the road bordering the woods. She was not there. I turned around, dragging myself weakly among the trees, my legs giving way under me. Then I saw her—in the same place! I crept back, tired, staggering, groping my way in the dark, taking long, light steps so she would not hear me. I would have wanted to have been able to scare her, surprise her, provoke her longed-for happiness and merriment. To start out together on our way, content with the fantastic day we had had, and ignore those two: Finlanda, lost in the horizon, and him following her, blinded by the flame of her hair.

I worked my way to the front of the tree where she sat, nestled against the leaves. Ready to shout my fury, shame, misery, disgust, and loneliness, and the terrors that were defeating us, degrading us, separating us, mocking us. But I had neither the time nor the strength once I saw her eyes and face, made strangely lambent by the darkness and her big, silent tears. She had surrendered too quickly, she was giving up, she had abandoned herself entirely to the tall forest that was quietly giving itself to night.

THE BALLS OF
FADED YARN

WE WERE coming back, behind the troops, to the places from which we had been driven. We stopped for months in a small town full of strangers, of children we didn't know, and it was best not to have anything to do with them.

We lived in one room, the strangers in another, and in between there was a hallway with a mosaic floor of bright, vibrant colors. I stared at it for whole minutes on end, my dirty fingernails digging into my flesh.

Alone, full of rage, I would look at the happy colors for a long time. I wanted to hit them with something, anything. Someday something terrible might happen.

The game the children were playing in the courtyard that day was wonderful, just exceptional, marvelous. But I quarreled with them, and they ran after me. After I'd crossed the stream and they realized they wouldn't be able to catch me, they called me names.

They had no way of knowing that every time I played with them it was to meet disaster head-on. Because they didn't understand this, and because they called me kike whenever they couldn't catch me, I picked up a screw. Through the curtain of tears that did not get the better of me, the colors of the mosaic danced: green, red, red, green, black. The screw whizzed fiercely through the air and hit the little girl. She dropped, felled, and turned pale, but less so than I.

I did not feel any of their blows. I only knew that they were forcing me to continue to fight, for I had not been able to save myself with just this outburst as I had hoped.

The penalty for attempting to escape my cage, or for anything else I had done, was to rid myself of envy. Oh, the exhausting watchfulness, the calculations! What protected me from envy and isolation was wickedness. No, not really wickedness. Something else, perhaps despair. After I'd hit the girl I was even angrier, because now I was forced to give them up; I could no longer wish to play with them. Caught between the safety and boredom inside and the excitement and wickedness outside, I could not find a place for myself.

In the afternoon the windows were covered with blackout paper; this spread a fluid calm that was suffocating. In the evening the knitting needles and eyeglasses would catch me between them. The blackout paper brought on the evening too quickly.

I would sit with my head between my hands like an old man. When I got tired of looking at the darkened windows, the eyeglasses, the blanket, the knitting needles, I would close my eyes and rehearse the strategy that gave me the strength to sleep and meet a new day. Without anyone noticing, I would slip under the table, bringing with me the wickedness, the noise, the cheerful hell of the outside. I knew then that I could wait.

She made me promise on her life that I wouldn't do it again. When she caught me the first time, I'd expected that, moved, she would stroke my hair. I had dreamed of this so much that, in my bewilderment, it took me a long time to realize that it hadn't happened the way I'd imagined. I had seen so clearly the moment when she would catch me—I knew she was bound to, because I could never guess exactly when she would come home—and I was sure she would smile sadly, pained by my bit of mischief, all too insignificant compared with the revenge I deserved. She would have won me over with that wistful smile of hers I dreamed so much about. She did not hit me. She didn't have time, she didn't have the strength, she loved me too much.

Had she smiled with understanding or with sorrow, or had she struck me, everything between us would still have been possible. But I heard her say to him: "In a few years that child will hit even me." I gasped for air, my arms flailing, horrified that she thought I was joking when I was trying to tell her I didn't know how to swim.

I couldn't find a place between the cruelty of those outside and the goodness of those inside—a place for me.

There were always more balls of yarn; as they became smaller, new ones appeared. Some large, some small. Round, dense. I could not bear to watch them shrink and become gloves, scarves, sleeves. I needed them to remain the way they were, I wanted to see them lined up one next to the other. They were not of a single color, but were faded, mixed, made of odds and ends. They produced a colorless knit, dull, thick, and resilient. At first I hid only one. Not the biggest. A medium-sized one, tightly wound, that bounced well.

The first time she saw me with it in the hallway she was surprised. She did not scold me; she took it away and told me not to touch them. They were colorless, but they caressed the colors of the mosaic. I would wait quietly, seemingly absentminded, for a chance to be alone, then I'd rush into the hallway, avenged for the games in the yard. She caught me again and asked for them back. By the third time she began to yell.

She swore that she would die if I continued; I knew it wasn't true, that she did not mean it.

When she set harsher, unfair rules that cut off any possibility of my coming close to her again, I began to stalk the colored ones. They appeared only rarely, a blue one, a red one. Once there was a green one too. I went after it, and hid it with an ordinary one in a spot I had chosen a few days before.

When it was first noticed missing, I walked calmly down the hallway, certain that I would soon be caught. But the colored ball of yarn that had been missing for three days and that had been the cause of so many arguments was not found in my possession. I was caught with an ordinary one, which was a lesser offense, even acceptable, now that the colored one was missing, the only colored one, the one that would have added a touch of beauty, and without which work came to a stop. Looking away, penitent and disdainful, I held out the ordinary ball of yarn as if it had never interested me at all.

Only several days later did the colored ball return to its place. Days went by, too, when there were no balls of yarn left and new ones hadn't appeared yet. Sleeves and fingers were piled up, strange scarves appeared, ugly sweaters, socks, boring gloves.

The noise in the yard started up again, tremendous. I regretted that I had not forgiven them for not accepting me, and that I had hit the little girl who was now running once more, blond and happy, among them.

The waiting became difficult, but it was no longer in vain. Sometimes the joy was particularly intense: the first ball of yarn to reappear was a colored one. A joy that was poisoned by the doggedness with which I had to wait for the appearance of the ordinary, mediocre balls, because only then could I regain it. They would reappear, and I could ignore once more, with a feeling of pride and superiority, both the hated noise from the courtyard and the subdued, muffled murmur of the knitting needles.

The pride I felt at never having been caught with one of the seductive, brightly colored balls gave me the confidence to see the noisy, foolish games in the yard as pitiful and petty. I had become strong, I counted on my pride, I had found it with difficulty, I had earned it slowly and carefully. I held onto it fiercely, with such grim, unprecedented, and unshakable determination, with such dogged, grim resolve, that I wanted to break open the door and hurl myself out like a madman.

PROUST'S TEA

THE PEOPLE crowding outside the big, heavy wooden doors, curious about the spectacle, were perhaps themselves travelers, or their companions, or loiterers of the sort often found in train stations, but on that afternoon not one of them was allowed into the waiting room. Nor could they see what was going on inside. The windows were too high, the rectangular glass panes in the doors too dirty and clouded with steam.

The waiting room was immense; it was hard to imagine anything bringing it to life; everything got lost, swallowed up in it. Crouched over their bundles, people in rags were huddling one on top of the other in clusters from the walls all the way to the center, filling up the room. The din was unending.

Shrill and desperate voices, hoarse voices, sometimes deep moans, grew suddenly louder when the nurses came by. The white uniforms barely managed to squeeze through the tangle of legs and bodies. Hands rose up all around to grab hold of the hems, the sleeves, even the shoulders, necks, and arms of these fine ladies. People were screaming, begging, groaning, cursing. Some were crying, especially those who were too far away and had lost all hope of getting a packet of food and a cup.

Those crowded on the other side of the wood and thick glass doors would have tried in vain to guess ages and sexes from the faces on the mass of skeletons, dressed in rags tied with string, that crammed into the waiting room. The women all looked like old, wretched convicts, and children with oversized skulls popped up all around them like apocalyptic men, compressed, stunted, as if an instrument of torture had shrunk them all.

The nurses knew, of course, that there were no men in the waiting room, nor young women. Had they understood the cries and the wailing around them, they would have realized that it was this very absence that aggravated the panic: the rescued did not understand, nor did they want to accept, that they had been saved. They suspected that this was a new ruse, even more diabolical, that would undoubtedly lead to new tortures, perhaps even to the end. Why else had the men and able-bodied young women been left behind? To bring them here later, on another train? Because there hadn't been enough room? Perhaps someone had objected to piling them on top of one another?

They could have done without those big, luxurious railway cars that swayed like imperial barges. They wouldn't have minded traveling in carts, walking for miles and miles, as long as they'd been allowed to stay together, husbands, wives, sisters, sons and daughters, the old and the children, all of them.

Shorn like the others, her head covered by some sort of burlap hood, the woman before whom the nurse had stopped was as ageless as the rest. She made no sound. She had not said a word when the person next to her had taken from her hands a piece of blanket and covered herself with it. She didn't flinch when the old woman on her left, sensing in her silence a confirmation of her own foreboding, became excited, raising her arms to the sky. Finally she lifted her head: a face shrunken, withered, old, like a Phoenician mask. But she didn't move, not even when the nurse passed by. She just kept watching, intense, like the midget resting his small yellowish head on her bare shoulder.

The air in the room quivered with heat. The continuous pulsing rumble of the mass lowered the ceiling and pulled the walls in closer. The hall had shrunk. Everything was happening close to the ground, at the height of the crowd. Only when you threw your head back and looked up did the ceiling recede, like a soaring, ever more unreachable sky. From the heights, the noise lagged, distant, weak, somewhere down below. Those who remained on the ground were deafened by it, drained by fear, oblivious to everything.

She, too, couldn't stop thinking about what might be happening on the train that never arrived. She couldn't have been allowed on board, she knew all too well that she looked like an old woman, no one would have believed that she was not yet thirty. But then she would have had no reason to want to be on the train for men and young women. Surely she too had seen how they had clung to each other without shame—my father and my cousin—the moment they left the lineup. She did not look at them, but without a doubt she had seen everything. Disciplined, she had joined her column, holding in her limp hand the hand of the midget trailing behind her. She didn't even yank at his arm as she helped him climb the high steps onto the train. She saw that the child, when he reached the top of the steps, had turned his wrinkled face toward the two who were left on the platform, sitting on the bench too close to each other. But the woman had not said a word; she sat down on the seat in the train and closed her eyes, exhausted.

Perhaps the commotion of so many confused voices coming from down below overwhelmed her, allowed her to forget, but suddenly she had turned around, pushing against the little midget's scrawny neck and dislodging him from his nest. In any event, her bony, dampish shoulder could not replace, even in the child's memory or dreams, the plump, fresh cheeks of the pillow he craved.

The hands that touched the neck and the matchstick arms of

the little savage were those of the lady in the white uniform. The lady was smiling at the little midget, bending over him, the red cross on her forehead shining, coming nearer. She held out the bag of biscuits and the tin cup.

The cup was hot. The little beast's cheeks bent over the yellowish liquid circle, into the fragrant steam. A pleasure that could not last; a pleasure one should not dare prolong, no matter what happiness one felt. An impossible pleasure, but real, because the hall was real too, and buzzing, and he heard the bag being ripped open over his head, and his hand filled with biscuits.

The boy sipped, numb with pleasure, frightened. He understood that everything was real and, therefore, that it would end; it was he, giddy with delight, who impatiently hastened its end. The cup was half emptied. He stopped drinking and looked at the stubby, fat biscuits in the palm of his hand. He began to nibble, patiently, on one of the grainy, sweet, scallop-edged shells. Only then did he feel hunger. He grabbed the bag with one hand. In the other he held the cup. He shoved a fistful of biscuits into his mouth. A little midget who inspired tenderness however ghastly he looked, and so the lady put an extra bag in his mother's hand.

"Drink the tea also. Drink, while it's still hot."

Perhaps the souls of those we've lost do indeed take refuge in inanimate objects. They remain absent until the moment they feel our presence nearby and call out to us for recognition, to free them from death. Perhaps, indeed, the past cannot be brought back on command, but is resurrected only by that strange, spontaneous sensation we feel when unexpectedly we come across the smell, the taste, the flavor of some inert accessory from the past.

But the aroma of that heavenly drink could not be reminiscent of anything; he had never experienced such pleasure. This magic potion could not, by any stretch of the imagination, be called "tea."

So it was necessary to look up toward the sky of dirty stone, where black clouds of flies swarmed, and where he expected Grandfather to appear, the only person who would have had an answer.

They had gathered, as usual, around him; everyone was holding his hot cup of greenish water infused with local herbs picked in those alien places, to which Grandfather would add, whenever he found them, acacia blossoms.

High up on the arched ceiling of the waiting room, where the light bulbs attracted billows of insects, Grandfather appeared as if on a round screen, and Grandmother, and his parents, and his aunt. They were warming their hands on the steaming cups, all of them staring at the same point high above, in front of them. Anda was there, too, of course. She took part, humble, submissive, but shameless enough, nevertheless, not to miss the tea ritual, to which Grandfather summoned everybody, some-times looking at each person a long time, letting each know that he knew everything about everybody, even about his son-in-law and this beautiful and guilty granddaughter.

Grandfather did not take his eyes off the little white cube of sugar that hung, as usual, from the ceiling lamp. They all had to stare at it intensely for some minutes before sipping the hot water. Those who remembered the taste of sugar, those, that is, who had had the time, before the disaster, to accustom their palates to the sweetness of the little white lumps, gradually felt their lips become wet and sticky. The brackish green drink became sweet, good, "real tea," as Grandfather would say.

The ceremony was repeated almost every afternoon, pre-sided over sternly yet not without a touch of humor by the old man, his unkempt beard mottled in black. He was convinced that he would return home, and he conserved as a symbol of that world, and for that world, a dirty sugar cube. While the boiling water was being poured, no one was allowed to look anywhere but in his own cup, and one waited to hear the water splash and bubble in the neighboring cup, until one by one all of them were filled. Then everyone raised his eyes toward the lamp from which a tiny parallelepiped of almost-white sugar hung on a string. They had to stare at it patiently for a long time, and had to sip the tea slowly, until everyone felt his lips, tongue, mouth, his entire being refreshed, mellowed by the memory of a world they must not give up, because, Grandfather firmly believed, it had not given them up and could not do without them. The tea steamed in the cups; everyone was silent, all concentrating, as they had been told to, on a small, dirty cube of sugar that Grandfather had had the idea to save and hang up in front of them every day.

Up there, above the din in which the poor wretches tried, uselessly, to return to another life, up there, in an open space, isolated from the huge waiting room, Grandfather, confident in a return that would not come to pass, could have assured them that the magic potion was indeed proof that the world had welcomed them back. But even this strange drink did not remotely resemble "real tea."

"Dunk the biscuits in the tea. Drink it while it's hot."

"Drink while it's hot," repeated now one woman, now another.

Dunked in the tea, the plump, round biscuits would have had the very flavor of happiness had there been time for surrender, this dizzying fullness of feeling—the priceless gift that only a chosen few can hope to deserve, and that someday must be repaid in a miraculous exchange.

The biscuits tasted like soap, mud, rust, burnt skin, snow, leaves, rain, bones, sand, mold, wet wool, sponges, mice, rotting wood, fish, the unique flavor of hunger.

There are, then, certain gifts whose only quality and only flaw is that they cannot be exchanged for anything else. Such gifts cannot, at some later time, be recalled, repossessed, or returned.

If, later, I lost anything, it was precisely the cruelty of indifference. But only later; and with difficulty. Because, much later, I became what is called . . . a feeling being.

WEDDINGS

A TOWN with dusty streets lined by giant, disheveled trees. Sunlight lingered in large, well-tended courtyards. The morning rose slowly; noon hovered, indolent, over the loud, seemingly endless lunch. So many and such unusual courses, slowed down even further by a knife and fork too heavy for the boy's greediness and impatience.

Evenings came swiftly. Families lined up in rows and chairs and benches in front of low white houses, recounting stories about the war until after midnight. The silence of the crystalline sky lent their voices a strange clarity and sadness.

They hadn't moved in yet with their other relatives on the outskirts of the small town. They still lived in the center with the teachers.

DAYLIGHT BURST suddenly, like an enormous orange balloon pierced by a shaft of light. Joyful young voices animated the main street. Windows flew open at the laughter and singing of the first groups that passed by. A Sunday, fresh and impetuous as there hadn't been before, stirred up the calm of the early morning streets. People wandered about, restless, perplexed; met, separated, sought each other out, converged.

It seemed that everyone, lured by the colors and excitement of the street, was outside. The columns of people kept getting bigger, overflowing the sidewalks, advancing in ever denser waves.

Pushed and carried by the crowd, he kept his balance by holding his cousin's hand.

The small town rose on a wave of anticipation. Entire convoys, compact rows of heads bobbed toward the park. There he would be giving his speech.

He would have liked to hurl himself into the midst of the exuberant, dancing crowd.

Walking tired him. They still knew nothing about his mission; the secret weighed on him. From all directions the wind carried the sound of loud voices, a deafening chorus. The sun filtered down in lazy rays, giving him vertigo.

His cousin dragged him along, occasionally squeezing his hand to remind him that he was still there. He understood that the boy was defending himself the way he usually did, with apathy. Efforts to make the boy tougher had failed, and finally, exhausted, he had resigned himself to the child's weakness and confusion.

Little by little, methodically, he tried to understand the boy's character. But he did not suspect how accustomed the boy was to withdrawing, as soon as he was figured out, and seeking new hiding places.

For the past month, since his acquisition of so many relatives in this unfamiliar town, the boy had been staying with his cousin, the teacher. A tender refuge, one might have thought, for from the start he cheerfully indulged the curiosity and kindness these people showed him. Soon after his arrival he had succeeded in forgetting the feeling of suffocation that had seized him at times in the past. His hosts were always ready to cheer him up, to please him with some surprise, keep him company.

Thus for almost a week they had prepared him with soothing words for the blue vitriol bath. They convinced him to associate the words "blue vitriol"—words that in fact seemed to belong to a foreign realm—with the miracle of his future growth, his becoming as big and strong as other children his age. The hypocrisy of his garrulous relatives hit him too late. Their deceitful words burned like scalding needles on his red, inflamed flesh. The water was boiling, stinging. His screams were to no avail, they held him down, determined, their tender smiles gone. Eventually, satisfied, they informed him that he was cured of his scabies.

He didn't feel the suffocation then. He felt it in the afternoon when he met with the teacher to rehearse his speech. He had learned to avoid each new trap as it was laid for him. He no longer made the mistake of believing he was secure among his own people. He warily observed the smug teacher so trusting in his own intuitions. The sessions with this cousin had turned into a game played by someone else; he no longer had reason to rebel.

Recent confrontations had taught him even more than the incident of the blue vitriol bath. At first he had let himself be deceived by the manly camaraderie—no baby talk, no hugging—that the teacher seemed to be offering. He waited for him, happy, as in a dream. So that it seemed only natural to answer the questions this newfound cousin kept asking him.

"Were you afraid there?"

"Yes, in the evening."

"Did they beat you?"

"Not often. I hid from them. I wasn't scared of them."

"What scared you, then?"

"The evenings. Beautiful evenings. Fields, fields, stretching as far as the eye could see. Very beautiful evenings."

"Is that what frightened you?"

"Yes. A desert all around. Crows. I don't know. Silence. The fields went on forever. The silence too."

The cousin paused.

"I see. You were terrified by the vastness of it all. And the others?"

"They prayed, they whispered. Some cried. I was alone."

"What was the hardest thing?"

"The food."

The conversations were followed by long walks, during which the teacher found out everything he wanted to know. Sometimes he wrote things in a notebook with a shiny blue cover that he would whisk out from his shirt pocket.

"Did you ever cry?"

"When Grandfather died. He was the closest to me."

"Were there happier days too?"

"Yes, when Mara got sick the first time. They took me to Uncle's so I wouldn't catch it."

The boy paid attention to him as to an older brother; he gave him his full trust. He forgot that the others, too, had walked him to the threshold of friendship, and then suddenly had revealed their true faces. They enjoyed the sight of the extreme suffering of others, it amused them. . . . He had forgotten, he didn't have the time to prepare himself and was caught unawares by this cousin's other face.

The speech sounded good; they practiced it every day. It contained everything he had told his cousin, but arranged differently; it was shorter, with new words. "Silence all around," he had said; it became "a vast silence," a great improvement even if he didn't understand it.

Then, suddenly, the teacher became harsh, turned cold and somber like a raven.

"It's no good, it's not good at all! You've got to speak louder! If you don't, nobody will hear you. Louder, louder, do you understand?"

This shouting caught him by surprise, paralyzed him. But he

quickly found his voice again, hoping to appease the maniac: "... our brothers, in whose hands we saw a loaf of bread, when we had forgotten what bread looked like. And we say to you, let us not forget, let us not forgive, let us punish those who ..."

"That's better. Once more now, let's hear it!"

As he grew more daring, the pitch of his voice rose too high, like a squawk. The ruler leaped in the air and landed on the table, crack!

"No, no, no! How many times do I have to tell you? You're lost in the clouds as usual. You're rushing just to get it over with! You must get the right intonation, do you understand? Enunciate, loudly.... Come on, try it again, starting with 'our brothers, in whose hands ...'"

Again and again the ruler hit the table in time with the desperate shouts of the little man, red with rage. The boy started again from the beginning, exhausted, with even less success.

He had to hold out his hand. The ruler came crashing down, ten times, like ice, on his fingers. The tears wouldn't come, just wouldn't, they gurgled in the depths. He held them back in time out of pity for himself. His throat was as tight as if he were being suffocated by smoke. He was splitting in two, he didn't care. Another self, detached from him, would cope with these sessions.

No one had ever struck him before. Not even the time when he had seen his father being led off at gunpoint and he had continued playing with the other children in the yard: they had called him "selfish." He didn't understand what the word meant, just felt its weight, the guilt, in his hurry to join the others, who were looking for smooth, flat pebbles to play ducks and drakes, stones that would hit the water with a smack and leap to the opposite bank of the river. Even then no one had hit him; he had never been hit until now.

The closer they got to the event, the more demanding became the rehearsals. Only the day before—since there was little hope of getting it right—his cousin had tried, with disarming stupidity, to revive their old friendship. He was joking, to show him that he could be at once young and old. . . .

Now the strange hand squeezed his absentmindedly. The teacher had neither the ability nor the sensitivity to revise and correct his earlier impressions of the boy. He would have been amazed were he aware of the calm detachment with which he was being observed. The boy had long since become skillful at shielding his feelings by retreating behind a pale mask of sleepiness. But at this particular moment he let himself go, living his experiences intensely. The teacher's presence had lost all power over him. He let himself be swept along by the frenzy of the crowd that was about to explode.

He watched the throngs in the park. Rebellious voices, festive voices. Youthful eyes, mirrors shimmering with the reflection of leaves still moist with dew. The teacher's hand seemed lifeless; he didn't catch his companion's mood.

A murmur ran through the foliage, then stillness hovered briefly over the park. But right away the railroad workers' brass band boomed a military march. A tall, very thin man with a large mustache got up on the improvised podium. He spoke of the war, of suffering in the camps, of peace, of retribution, justice, labor.

Behind the stage the small hero waited his turn. He was to speak right after the officer, before the woman. His cousin's hand, forgotten on the crown of his head, suddenly propelled him in front of the crowd.

They lifted him up and stood him on a chair. The crowd's excitement grew. Then they abandoned him in front of the seething multitude. He was not afraid that he would forget the order of the words or the proper intonation. He was terrified that the chair might fail him, that it would overturn and pitch him forward into the pit.

They were waiting for him in total silence. He felt their eagerness, their ravenous hunger. Pulling himself together, he met them head-on.

"We, who haven't known the meaning of childhood, nourished by cold and fear, under the mantle of war, we turn, today . . ."

He didn't see their veiled eyes, their tears. Applause, bravos—he rallied, haggard and drained.

Behind the podium the cousin accepted congratulations. His embarrassed face indicated that the speech had lived up to his expectations, its success was deserved. As for the little actor, he was passed from the arms of one relative to another, then to the acquaintances. The avalanche of embraces wore him out. The solicitude with which he was treated relieved him. They kept asking him again and again if they could get him anything, if he wanted anything, their words and gestures hesitant, as if they were afraid to hurt his feelings.

For a long while afterward the hero could still feel the crown of laurels on his head. Numerous privileges that he now enjoyed reminded him of his triumph.

His cousin, the teacher, now consented to become the comrade he had been in the past. He sought other outlets for his intransigence and zeal. He thought that surely the boy would have forgotten the harshness with which he had treated him; after all, experiences of that sort served to build character. They started going on long evening walks again and having many conversations. Everything could be just as before. . . .

Still, ostensibly the event was not forgotten. They recalled it at every opportunity. Indeed, they seemed to look for opportunities to bring it up, and each time they found one they seemed to become more and more familiar with the great event; they even started to act proprietary toward it, with the growing conviction that it somehow belonged to them.

People would stop dead in the street to take a look at the precocious celebrity. Acquaintances, or even complete strangers, would cross from the other sidewalk and walk up to the white-haired lady:

"Excuse me, but isn't that the boy who gave the speech?"

They patted him on the head. He would feel, for an instant, as if a golden power were ennobling his shoulders. Then it would be over. He would be yelled at because he did not say hello to the tobacconist's fat wife, because his fingernails were dirty, or there he goes again, putting his hands in his pockets, he looks elsewhere, doesn't pay attention when grown-ups talk to him. . . .

Nothing upset him more than the compliments of relatives, particularly of those who lived far away and had not participated in the event, but were impressed by the mere echo of his fame.

"But my dear, why don't you come to see us? . . . I've heard . . . of course, bring him over at least once. I beg you. . . ."

During these visits, in houses of people he did not know, the hero was served up right after the dessert. Tears were shed and immediately forgotten in the chatter and the shouting, as each guest tried to drown out the next. Afterward coffee was served, weak and sweet.

AN EVER-GREATER number of new acquaintances turned up—wives of cousins three times removed, former neighbors of the cripple who delivered seltzer water, childhood friends of deceased grandparents. People looked for each other, trying to recapture the old life, the old pleasures.

The winds of hope shook the little town during these first

months of peace. They lived loudly and with excess vitality. The lust for life constantly sought reasons to break out and often did without any reason.

The parks rustled with tango rhythms. Visits, birthdays, name days, anniversaries, parties, engagements, weddings. Especially weddings. Weddings of relatives and acquaintances, of neighbors, friends, and friends of friends, innumerable weddings. They went everywhere they were invited, as if to make up for lost time and reassure themselves that they had come back alive, that they could start over again with renewed strength. The whole family went, no one was left behind, neither the old nor the children.

. . . It would be hard to say whose idea it was. Somehow, it was in the air. People kept looking for something new, exciting, something to stoke the fire, to provoke tears, laughter. Never mind who was the first to suggest it—they seized it instantly, casually. The boy went along without reacting.

He still remembered the first time he had felt as though smoke were choking him: he couldn't breathe, and then he seemed to split in two. The soldier had given him a quarter of a loaf of bread. Grandfather's and Mother's livid faces appeared in the doorway, astonished. He had returned victorious. They could hardly believe their eyes; but they forbade him ever to go near a soldier again. A part of him, the part drawn toward friendship with the soldier, was gradually torn away from him. In the following weeks, tortured by hunger, the boy often felt as though he were choking from smoke. But he became accustomed to it and learned to face it calmly.

He was jolted from his plunge into the past by the percussionist's bang on the drums. The dance stopped, the couples separated. The time for tears had come.

"Quiet, everybody! Quiet, please! We have a guest of honor!"

They stood him on a chair or on a table. The wedding guests got their handkerchiefs ready. Near the door, a young man caressed his girlfriend's shoulder. When the applause broke out, he drew her closer to him.

Up on his podium, the guest of honor recited his lines. His white shirt collar lit up his pale face, its delicate features blurred with fatigue. The stinging smoke choked him only rarely now. The split occurred painlessly. It was someone else who stood in front of him, who recited the same pathetic speech. He had become used to what was happening to him.

Applause and embraces followed. The newcomers repeated the gestures of the guests at previous parties. Those who had accompanied him to other weddings—close relatives or the habitual partygoers—were already familiar with his act, and they smiled at him conspiratorially.

He could escape the gushing and the pawing only when he finally found himself in front of a gigantic slice of wedding cake. They also brought him a small glass of wine. The musicians, he noticed, were given larger ones. It was his habit to withdraw into a corner near the orchestra.

Forgotten near the instrument cases, lost in the melodies, he would slide back into the past, among once-familiar faces: Grandfather's, before the sickness struck him, as he laid his large old hand on his shoulder . . . the doctor's as, in tears, he stood by the bridge during that first night of plundering, after they had been attacked and dragged off the freight cars, their clothing, their rings, everything they still owned taken away from them.

Only Uncle and a very few others had been able to hold on to some money. He must have taken plenty of cash with him and hidden it so well that he still had it even after all the searches and beatings they had endured. He had managed to keep the money; you could tell by the large slices of bread and jam he would buy. People would give a coat for two slices of bread, but that wouldn't worry him. From time to time, he came to them, nevertheless, to borrow money. Not much, small sums, for a few days. He never spent any of it, obviously, and he always returned it on time. But when Mara got sick they put a stop to his little game.

"What are you doing here? What are you thinking about?"

A heavy hand rested on the nape of his neck. Every now and then a reveler would discover him behind the double bass, startling him out of his trance. He would pick up the boy and hand him back to his family or drag him to the head table, forcing the bride to grant him the first dance of the evening, as a mark of respect. The groom would nod his consent.

Attempts were made to silence the crowd, but the buzzing persisted. Chairs were pushed to one side, the band blew a long fanfare. The bride strode to the center of the floor to honor the famous guest. She led him gently, bending over him from time to time with a smile. The music did its part while he hurried and counted the steps, one to the left, two to the right; sometimes he would trip over the long train, or the buckle and black shiny tongue of his shoe would get caught in the veil. The dance with the bride was not so much the high point of the evening as an interlude. He saw people chatting in groups, distracted, faces flushed from too much food and drink.

Occasionally his oratorical skill was rewarded by a talk with the bride's father-in-law, who would make room next to himself at the head of the table, trying to look wise as he marveled at the hero's precocity.

But, carried away by music and drink, they soon forgot him, and he returned to sit by the saxophone case. The musicians toiled conscientiously, arousing desire and spreading gaiety. The hall heated up; a haze of perspiration rose on clouds of dust.

The boy withdrew behind the percussionist; he rocked on the legs of the narrow, rickety chair and leaned his back against the wall. Frenzy mounted, they chatted and chatted, they recalled the dead and the suffering. They cried, flung money at the orchestra, clamored for horas and romantic tunes, fell into one another's arms.

Uncle had looked at Mara, ravaged by illness. He expressed sorrow for their misfortune. And then he asked them, with a certain bashfulness, to lend him some money, just for one day, just until tomorrow. Mother did not answer him; she was seething. He was her brother, but he had reached bottom, she couldn't stand him any longer. She didn't answer him, not the second nor the third time around, and he asked again and again in rising embarrassment. She simply looked into his eyes. Only after a while, in a tired voice, she said to him, "Sit here for a bit." Uncle stooped and, humiliated, did as he was told.

Half an hour later, Uncle took him along to stay with him for two weeks, to give Mara time to recover and to avoid contagion. Uncle had behaved toward him with unusual kindness. He had succeeded in getting a blanket for the boy's exclusive use. He slept rolled up in it like a bag and no longer felt the cold floor at night. For two whole weeks he even had enough food. Uncle brought him bread, spoiled him, protected him, frowned at his wife whenever she showed resentment at the attention their guest was enjoying. But the tensions surrounding Uncle had exhausted him, and he wished that all would be over soon so that he could return home.

"Hello there, sir, why are you all by yourself? Come on, let's go see the little monkey. . . ."

This time it seemed it was a bris. He shouldn't have hid from the start; it didn't last long. He knew the rituals of the various festivities, there were so many of them.

Once he woke up around midnight. His speech raced through his mind; he looked as through fog at the confusion in the room, the sour mood of the hungover couples. He realized that his act must have been over a while ago, that it was probably the moment to approach the bride, that is, if he had executed the earlier part of the program. He stumbled sleepily to the head of the table and found himself face to face with a roly-poly grandmother in a white gown, with a flower wreath, bloated features, flour and syrup mingled into sweat running down her pasty face. This time it was not a real wedding but an anniversary, he now remembered . . . a silver wedding anniversary. Too late—the old bag had spotted him. Hastily she welcomed him, smiled at him with her big metal teeth, impatiently reached over to him with gravy-stained hands. The remains of a slice of wedding cake were melting on the dessert plate in front of her. She insisted that he eat it and offered him her lipstick-smeared spoon. . . . He also saw the pickles, the chicken leftovers, the rice drenched in tomato sauce, the deep bowl of whipped cream. Swaying with nausea, he groped his way back to his corner by the orchestra and clutched tightly to his chair. They raised him onto his feet with difficulty—he had fallen suddenly in his sleep and the room was topsy-turvy, as though after an earthquake—and he had another round with the old bride. Next morning his family found him in bed at the neighbors', where he had been dropped off.

"Come, let's go, it's morning."

Other parties, other weddings. From now on everything will be different, they said, but, as though afraid of some impending calamity, they couldn't hold back. Something impelled them to recoup their energy and start all over again. The frail boy up on the chair touched them; the words of his speech bolstered their determination.

The young speaker lived up to expectations. Sometimes his speech was scheduled for the conclusion of a party, sometimes it was overlooked altogether. The hero would always sneak away to the musicians' corner. He felt at ease in their company.

A new morning dawned, his legs moved unsteadily, cool air soothed his eyelids. It was as if his other self wanted to split away again, as when Uncle came to borrow money to forestall them from doing the same, or when he guiltily stretched out his hand and his cousin, the teacher, gave him a blow that felt as though it would cut off all his fingers.

At parties he had always looked for his cousin, hoping to see him, at least once, mellowed by food and drink. But he never showed up. They said that the teacher was "off his rocker," he disappeared from home for days, even weeks, at a time, roaming the countryside with bands of rebels, unafraid of hunger or hardship. He had grown gaunt, emaciated, and each time he returned, they said, he could hardly wait to get going again.

The boy relived that extraordinary morning, the banners and flags, the men's lively glances, the streets dipped in gold, the festive riot in the park. He had fallen right into the bubbling, scalding applause, his skin red and swollen . . . no, no, that was another time, when they cured him with blue vitriol, held him fast so he couldn't escape. He remembered how he had drawn away from his cousin, bit by bit, when his friendship turned out to be a trap. From then on he was always on his guard.

Evening had come again. Candles and light bulbs illuminated the ballroom; the pale bride stood smiling at her father-in-law's side.

His friends the musicians gave the signal: a mighty beat on the big drum, two blows with the flat of the hand on the cymbals, and the hall fell silent.

"And now, a surprise: our own young . . ."

A chair was set up in place, the audience regrouped. The soloist was lifted and placed on the pedestal.

"We, who haven't known the meaning of childhood . . ."

Afterward—a slice of wedding cake, a small glass of wine, the horrors of the past. The nights, dragged out until dawn, flowed slowly; it took a long time for their dregs, and the thick, murky voices around him, to settle down. Then morning came. A spring day again, soft breezes blowing on tender eyes, and the boy offered the crowd his feelings, his old, choking fears.

The sky sparkled like a new knife. Only at dawn did he feel the smoke choking him again. He reeled, dizzy with weariness and sadness.

THE EXACT
HOUR

THE SHOPKEEPER liked novelties and jokes. Slightly cuckoo patrons brightened up his days. Cuckoos, but obvious cuckoos. The surly ones, he was convinced, had much worse things to hide.

When the shop door opened and the bell rang, Mr. Albu would raise a serene face, ready to hear the latest gossip or a good joke. He would weigh the empty bag; without rushing he would scoop the candy, then weigh the loaded bag and wait for the scale's pointer to stop quivering. He had refused to sell to a number of clients their favorite candies, confessing that they were not the freshest. Instead he recommended a new variety, a bit more expensive, true, but special, very special, unique, he repeated several times, his voice warm and deep.

He wouldn't have laughed at the thought that someone could think that a *radio* is a cage for electrocuting mice and frogs; he would have understood that *marzipan* could be a skinny animal that leaps across the fields on its three legs.

But he had never been forced to leave. Mr. Albu had remained home. He had had the luxury of growing with things and with words, of coming to terms with them. Like all people

59

who hadn't been torn from their rhythm and environment, he had a healthy confidence in what he knew. He couldn't imagine what chaos an unknown word could unleash in certain minds. Nor did he ever ask himself what other people were thinking. The craziness of mutes was, of course, more serious, but of no interest to him. He couldn't understand that a *table lamp* could be a large, heavy red boat floating on the water, that *Madagascar* could be a tree from which you picked hand grenades, that an *alarm clock* could be a black drill with saw-blade spirals.

Nevertheless, he accepted the strangest things. But he had to hear them, see them, be warned, become accustomed. For example, that very afternoon he would host, of all things, his daughter's first caller.

Sitting behind his counter, less excited than his wife but still amused by the child's turmoil, he had put on an air of easygoing indulgence. He smiled from time to time, resting on his elbows.

He was listening to the intense preparations going on next door. A girl's parents, he pondered, and the girl herself, often prefer exactly such a boy, calm, quiet, acquainted with suffering. He found it strange that he wasn't bothered by this observation.

The boy and his parents had been staying for some time at the home of the high school principal. Their being blood relations, it was said, had something to do with it.

Mr. Albu had already seen the suitor. When it was his turn to receive the school prizes, the young stranger had been slow in approaching the podium, still dazzled by the girl who had preceded him. Miss Albu had also noticed the boy's confusion, his pallor, his tension as he accepted the award, which was too heavy for his thin arms.

It was clear that this boy was not the picture of strength or energy. The girl said that no one had asked them to treat him with kid gloves. From the very beginning, they had eyed him with great curiosity. He had earned recognition: he read well, with a strange intonation that had the class mesmerized; as for mathematics, he was truly amazing—he shot out the answer, no need to work it out on paper. He had shown up, from God knows where, at the very end of the school year. Had it been necessary to eliminate a prize, it would have been more appropriate to exclude her rather than the stranger, said the impassioned girl. It was not true that they had raised the number of prizes to six to include him too. The newcomer, she insisted, deserved his prize. True, six first prizes did seem like a lot. But you had only to know the principal to be convinced that no one would receive what he did not deserve. Withdrawn, modest, her new classmate did not mix with the others, it was not his ambition to be first, she shouted out in defense of her protégé.

At the ceremony Mr. Albu had seen the boy's parents sitting, withdrawn, at the back of the hall. They looked as is expected of people who have been through the terrible things they were said to have endured. Skin and bones. You could also see the weakness and terror in the feeble gestures of the prizewinner. Mr. Albu had to admit that it was the stranger's seriousness that set him apart from the other children.

If, as was his habit, he had been looking through the shop window instead of facing the shelves, the shopkeeper would have realized that his guest still found the streets, houses, and signs of the little town bewildering. Having finally reached the store, he stopped cold and leaned against the brass rail below the sign that said ROZINA CANDY SHOP. He had come from Radaseni Street, having crossed Hala Street and walked down Beldiceanu Avenue. For a long time he stood there watching a wagon loaded with crates of shiny tomatoes that was teetering along behind an old gray horse with a long, dirty mane. The young man looked stupefied.

Bent over his boxes, hearing only the voices coming from the other room, the shopkeeper did not see him. "Dust the lamp." "Straighten out the bedspread." "Should I put on my pink ribbon?" "There's dirt on the alarm clock." "And on the radio." "Quick, the small table, the grandfather clock, and the radio." "Did you bring the puff pastry? Bring out more truffles and Turkish delight. Yes, and the fritters too. And the marzipan."

His back turned to the door, Mr. Albu did not see that the guest had reached for the doorknob. Standing on his tiptoes, using all his strength, he pushed.

The door opened a quarter of the way, setting off the bell. He stepped back, startled, taken by surprise. He stood on the threshold, his hand on the partially open door, deafened by the sound of so many bells descending on his shoulders.

"Come in, young man, courage. Come in."

He had entered without releasing the pressure on the handle, and the bell kept ringing. But Mr. Albu was already at his side. Patting his guest's brittle and plastered-down hair, he gently disengaged the boy's hand from the handle. The door swung shut and the sound magically ceased, swallowed up by a long and difficult silence.

"Almost elegant. Neat, in any case, well put together," the shopkeeper noted. The candidate had, indeed, been carefully groomed. Freshly polished sandals, clean white socks. His wide blue shorts floated lazily around his thin little legs. He even had a belt, and in almost good condition. A white shirt, short wide sleeves to his elbows, a closed collar tight around his long, yellowish neck. His hair was parted on the left, flattened in place by a wet brush—a skullcap, one could say. A wide-eyed, persistent look.

The shopkeeper too, in honor of the event, wore under his stiff white pharmacist's smock a new blue shirt and a silvery-white polka-dotted tie. He was trying out a part that, he knew, he wouldn't actually play until many years later.

He led the guest up the two steps to the rooms in the back of the store and opened the door wide for him. He remained behind and let some time pass before joining the others.

The departure of the enchanting creature, her choice of another protector, would be a sad event, the rotund Mr. Albu had to be telling himself, in his wisdom, as he pulled down the shades and closed up the shop. He imagined the visitor, or another many years later, saying hello, and again hello, bending over to kiss Madame Albu's hand, then going, choked with emotion, to sit next to the young lady.

The shopkeeper came into the room a good ten minutes later. The guest was sitting, confused, in front of a plate of sweets. He was unable to look at his hosts.

The master of the house understood immediately. His wife, Sophie, was leaning against the green terra-cotta stove, her arms behind her head. Soft clinging red dress, wide leather belt, black hair gathered into a bun, languor, the radiance of her soft, white neck . . . Mr. Albu understood why the guest did not feel at ease.

His daughter was wearing the same white silk dress she had worn at the prize ceremony. Thick dark braids, intense eyes. Fragile, stunning, attentive to the young caller.

Mr. Albu turned his gaze toward the mistress of the house. He had eyes for nothing else; he didn't notice that the boy had averted his eyes from the terra-cotta stove and was hesitating in front of the sweets. Nevertheless the shopkeeper seemed to understand what was happening, and to guess what would follow.

"Take a fritter first," suggested the woman.

The boy was startled. He closed his eyes and held on to the word; he saw *fritters*, little brown lizards with long greenish tongues spurting poison. *Fritters*, hundreds of them, jumping up suddenly through the tall, thick grass—too late to protect himself from their thin, icy hiss.

Albu seemed to have realized that the guest could not accept words calmly, even if he understood them; Sophie was too close and her voice was burning the air. He would have liked to set the boy more at ease, but the mistress of the house had decided to ignore the guest's shyness; she had no idea that she was speaking to him in another tongue. She kept coming closer, driving the boy crazy with her protectiveness and warmth.

"Tell me, how did you become so good at mathematics? I've been told that they moved you directly into an advanced class."

Mr. Albu waited for the echo of her words to die down. The shopkeeper then repeated his wife's words, convinced that, this time, the guest would hear them. He hoped in this way to gain the boy's confidence.

"He's not stupid, only a little slow," the host was probably thinking to himself, happy that the boy had seized the rope thrown at him and answered right away, speaking very rapidly to gain some time.

As the boy caught his breath, Madame Albu commented, in a precious tone, how *interesting* she had found his story about his grandfather, about how the old man had taught him to read and write. The guest struggled to regain his breath; Albu slid the plate under the boy's nose, indicating what was expected of him.

"Help yourself—take this one, it looks good."

The boy didn't close his eyes again to see the lizards dart every which way; he managed a smile out of the corner of his mouth in complicity with his father-in-law. Mr. Albu considered this the key moment of the evening. The high point of the visit—he had no way of knowing it then—would prove, however, to be something else.

After the prizewinner had eaten enough fritters, the lady of the house attacked again.

"Take some *marzipan* too. It's very good."

The stranger stared at the dish in confusion; he saw the animal leaping across wide pastures, its thick tail touching the ground at intervals like a third foot. The *truffles* had not been mentioned yet, with their velvety skin and big, watery eyes, rubbing themselves against the bark of trees, delicately raising their grass-moistened snouts to sniff the air; he had not met the *raisins*—flies, of course, disgusting, lazy, tame, warm; no mention yet of *peanuts* chirping among the branches.

As could be expected, Mr. Albu held his breath. It was a miracle, a *divine* intervention, he would say later: in his ignorance the boy had put his hand right on the *marzipan*. His eyes were shut, his fingers tightened around the thick tail of the animal, gasping as he lifted a now even paler face and, come what may, smiled at them.

Her dark braids swinging, the fiancée turned on the *chandelier;* then Rozina suggested, her radiant head in the light, that they turn on the *radio.* The guest heard nothing but the high-pitched voice of the mistress of the house, *sublime,* you have *sublime* ideas, Rozie; the little girl approached the radio, the cage, and turned it on, and the material covering the front of it began vibrating as if the rodents inside had wakened suddenly. The radio warmed up, until finally it released a human voice.

"The time is exactly . . ."

Then they looked at the blue glass fish vibrating on top of the box. The *alarm clock* and the fabric covering the face of the *radio* vibrated to the same fine rhythm until the gong struck.

". . . six o'clock."

The melody rose thinly in the room. Small musicians, no bigger than pins, with even smaller instruments the size of pencil tips. The first violinist was looking carefully through two thick lenses each as big as the eye of a needle. An invisible orchestra was amassed in a corner of the cage, where the tiny mice were being carried away by an electric minuet. The miracle of the orchestra hidden in the box lasted about half an hour—but this was not yet the climax to the evening. Then Madame Albu addressed Rozina:

"Why don't you light the *table lamp*."

The boy expected the hollow boat jostled by the turbulent waters to catch fire, but they couldn't have known that; they pushed several buttons, but this wasn't the high point of the evening either, no more than it had been at the beginning of the visit when Madame had put her hands up behind her neck, nor when the *fritters*, the *truffles*, the *raisins*, and the *peanuts* had been deployed or the *marzipan* had come crashing down.

It wasn't going to be easy to forget all this. It was something else that he would remember for too many years afterward. The atmosphere became more relaxed; everything became more and more natural. Mr. Albu realized perfectly well that he could never accept this candidate. In the end he had succeeded in pinpointing him with some accuracy. "Sympathetic, no doubt, but not for us," would have commented the good rotund man.

Having already settled the account, the shopkeeper was no longer looking at his guest when the *exact hour* was announced. He did not see the amazed expression on the boy's face while he watched them, Rozina included, check their watches and turn the little star-shaped wheels. None of them went to adjust the *alarm clock*; placed as it was directly on the *radio*, it was apparently self-regulating. Even if he had foreseen how many years the boy would carry such a nonsensical notion with him—that all *alarm clocks* placed on radios were self-regulating through simple contact, and always showed the exact time—Mr. Albu still wouldn't have had anything to add to his conclusion at the end of the visit: "I'd like to see him in ten years."

* * *

HE WOULD have found him in the capital, just entering the cool
hall of an elegant apartment building on the corner of Batişei
and Vasile Lascăr. By now, no doubt, in addition to other
wonders he had figured out the mechanism that told the exact
time. Over ten years one gradually acquires a certain confidence in manipulating words; time begins to flow normally, as
it does for those who haven't been shaken. He nods to the
concierge, the concierge nods in return

He went to the elevator and pushed the button.

He had developed a way with words, a certain familiarity;
now he identified objects, situations, moods, and functions by
name. Even if words maintained a distance that often made
them seem vague, contradictory. As if it were possible, at any
time, to question their existence or to interchange them without
disturbing the balance, the chaos, the fog in which they
evolved. In which he also evolved, in an almost unreal way. As
if events were likely to abandon him at the very moment he
came close to them. A game once more: he will wake up
confused, in a void, unable to recognize himself, or he will
never wake again, which would change nothing.

Perhaps this explained why he was always on time wherever
he went. When the elevator came down he looked at his watch.
Three minutes to eight. This punctuality was also a reason why
Mr. Alfandari could not stand him. But it reassured him; it gave
him a kind of security—a focus—a reprieve, even a protection.

Lately, Mr. Alfons Alfandari no longer hid his distaste; he
was becoming more and more convinced that Rita was sleeping with her classmate. The young woman often came home
late, slipping in after midnight, on tiptoes. Sometimes he did
not even hear her; maybe she hadn't come home at all. Of
course, the only thing that bothered him was the young man

she had chosen. He could not tolerate shy types; the polite, quiet, punctual ones always had something to hide. He suspected, in fact, that this provincial boy was not at all polite, quiet, shy, punctual, but just the opposite. These tomcats, he was convinced, ended up exploding with incomparable ferocity.

Especially since, for about a month now, his daughter had stopped going out. She kept her light on until very late at night, and in the morning she would appear, haggard, her mind elsewhere. Her eyes remained fixed to the telephone. Her face white, desperate for days on end, until at last she might hear the awaited voice. Crazy conversations, more silences than anything else.

Her back turned, rifling distractedly through a dresser drawer, as she usually did when she was plotting something, the young woman brusquely informed Alfons about the party. He did not answer. After all, he was used to her parties ever since high school; the fact that she was now involved with all kinds of people was none of his business. She turned suddenly, and he saw her face. She looked unwell; that shy type was torturing her.

"As you wish, darling. I won't be here. There is a bridge game at Mitu's."

"I'd like it better if you stayed," the daughter insisted.

Alfons would have loved to be rid of that dubious young man. Rita had always been rather extravagant; perhaps with a weakness for the bizarre. These fellows unsure of their own desires, as though their insides were being eaten away. His punctuality could be more than just provincial gaucheness. . . .

The elevator had reached the third floor; the guest looked at his watch once more. One minute to eight. He certainly could have waited for at least a few minutes in the hallway. A little lateness is normal—it was even demanded by the large silver plaque on the door that announced: Alf Alfandari.

His beard freshly trimmed, the distinguished Alfons appeared at the door, cold but civil, in a light gray suit that emphasized his slenderness. He shook the guest's hand.

"Come in, my dear, come in, courage."

The host's rich voice was drowned out by the pendulum clock. Eight o'clock. "Not bad, rather well groomed," Mr. Alf Alfandari was saying to himself. A relatively new suit, navy blue, freshly pressed. Had Madame Alfandari still been alive, the student might possibly have found an ally in her. Withdrawn, quiet, suffering the blows of married life in silence, she would have gotten along with her son-in-law; she would have discovered—God knows—qualities in him.

While rapidly patting down his bushy, wavy hair, the young man from the provinces saw Rita's father examining his shoes in the mirror. Worn, true, but well waxed with shoe polish until they shined. Perhaps shined too much.

Rita was waiting for him in her soft and supple cherry-red dress. Her black hair was gathered at the top of her head to uncover her delicate neck. Her hands crossed languidly behind her head, she pressed herself against him uninhibitedly. She looked at him for a long time, pale, waiting for forgiveness, commitment, a declaration, anything. For nearly a year now she had let herself be charmed and tortured by this boy. It shocked Alf, she knew it. He still said that she would find an adventurer, that she needed an adventurer . . . as incredible as it may seem, this boy himself is proof of that. She will find one, Alf insisted stubbornly.

One by one, other friends arrived. Alf smiled and looked at them as if they were a bunch of gadflies. So, it was with this bunch that Signorina Rita was involved, all these guys who dreamed of nothing better than getting an engineering job somewhere.

As had been agreed, Lică showed up later. Shaking with cold in a ragged windbreaker. In ski boots, as he had discussed with his cousin, the fiancée. But by then the master of the house had already left for his bridge game.

The party became more and more animated, and there was a lot of drinking. Expensive stuff, too, you could tell by the taste. They staggered, minds on fire, ever dizzier, too young for such expensive liquor.

If they could have seen their faces as they would be in another ten years, scattered to the four winds, then they would see Rita with her distinguished Mr. Waler or Mr. Wilkinson, and Lică in Mexico or in Madagascar, as he had always dreamed. Maybe if they had met somewhere, Lică would have told her what had happened that night, and Lady Winston would have laughed to tears. Remember the *bidet*, ha-ha, ha-ha, what a wonderful, crazy youth, a country more and more forgotten, strange, ha-ha, hahahaha, so he didn't know what it was for, hahaha, the symbol of another world, hahaha, that's why he ran off then, disappeared without a trace, that lunatic . . . that restlessness, ha-ha . . . their crazy youth, he had taken it with him, surely he must have remained the same adolescent, a frail despot, candid, unpredictable ha . . . ha . . . ha. But Lady Wellington would have stopped abruptly, her face gone white, her eyes staring at the sky. Such is life. When you least expect it you find yourself suddenly face to face for a fraction of a second with another being, burst from heaven, from hell, real, bewildering. And Lică would have looked away, respecting the silence, the truth that the woman had discovered. Whatever had happened in the meantime, whether he got to Mozambique or Monaco, Lică had not lost his sense of decency, his extraordinary tact, his modesty. A crazy, rowdy colossus, a brawler, ready for anything, in short a terrific guy, he had never lost his tact, that's for sure.

That evening the cousins went into the luxurious bathroom together. Being the more sober, Lică managed to close the door and lock it with the key. Then he located the switch next to the door, the light above the sink went on. He turned it again, and the chandelier came on. The bathroom was gigantic—it overwhelmed them, they didn't know what to do. The green bathtub with its separate levels, the white closets, the pink sink, a gilded shower behind a waterproof blue curtain. Jars, brushes, bottles, the round yellow sponge, the square red washcloth. They stumbled around, dizzy, amid this splendor—they couldn't remember why they were there. They could not find their bearings; there was simply too much space.

They found themselves in front of two white porcelain bowls. They looked identical, even though one was narrower, with silver faucets. There should have been a sign, an explanation, a guide—there were still plenty of uninitiates about.

They bent over the bowls. Lică understood that his cousin was not yet drunk enough—he knew him too well. Whatever he is he's *pudique*, no doubt about it. They had opened their flies with their right hands, both of them fumbling with their buttons. They were leaning over bowls that looked identical.

The radio fell silent; they'd turned out the lights in the apartment and couples were dancing in the dark, without music.

Self-conscious, not to see, not to hear, the two were leaning further and further over their right hands, as though to shield themselves. Timid, confused, solitary rebels. Furious orphans, wild animals blinded by the jungle. But they had nothing to do except, with a preoccupied air, examine their watches.

TALE OF THE
ENCHANTED PIG

The hugs, the groaning and moaning, God, they were unreal!
These people we had come back to looked healthy, their houses
were prosperous, their kids well fed and full of fun. And we
were still alive, famished, ready to have a good time, as if the
whole world were going to be ours. Older, but saved, we had
arrived just as the good weather was letting us know it was here.
We were easy to fool, childish, like the wind of those spring
months. As if five years had disappeared without a trace.

When they think about the place and the time of that unbelievable return, others perhaps remember only the light that
burst over the streets.

We hadn't come back on a magic carpet. For long months
we had straggled along, dizzy with the roar of artillery, ravaged
by hunger, behind the troops. But time had shrunk; in the end
it seemed like an instant's flight over the golden bridge between
two worlds. No one had had a chance to get ready for meeting
the other realm.

Faces, houses, flowers, new words, songs, parks, and families
suddenly surged on us. A noisy, demonstrative, keening world

had sprung out of the earth to claim us, certain from the very first of our kinship. And so the first food, clothes, bed, the first gifts. And then the first reproaches; the guy with the mustache, who claimed he was a godfather, had offered nothing but a pillow; so-and-so, a cousin of grandmother's, had handed over only an old teapot, while another, a tall clown with glasses from whom no one had expected anything, had come loaded with dresses, shirts, shoes, even some candlesticks.

THE WONDER of a hamlet living on a cloud, with white peaceful houses, lost under the manes of long-haired trees, on streets where undulating coaches rolled by. A metropolis! A fairy tale!

Amazement at the miracles and the stillness and terror of a house; enchantment because it was *that* house; amazement, wonder, and fear of what was happening inside it.

The slow hours, the sinking into the sofa. The angles, the colored criss-crossing of so many straight lines, magic reflections on the edge of the mirror that had not been fathomed yet; neither had the wheels of the bicycle, nor the shrieks that pierced holes in the walls like bullets.

The sofa, the ceiling, and the strip of window were stained by the red from the street. Through the curtain sunlight fell in round bloody flames.

Sometimes you caught sight of the sharp corners of the walls, the arches over the doors, the opaline and square ceiling, its corners pink and green with fly specks, so many unexpected images left by dust spots on the old paint; the glint—just an instant long—of the drapery rings. Then the chairs around a field of notebooks, slide rules, T-squares, and colored chalk.

In the mirror lightning flashed: parallels cut by a transversal. And soon you heard, coming from far away, unfamiliar new words: *Parallels cut by a transversal, the concurrence of bisectors. The geometric locus of the intersection of the medians of an isosceles triangle inscribed in . . .* The words got closer. Medians, pyramids, arcsine alpha. The colored straight lines out of which came thin snakes called beta, cotangent. Sometimes you heard washed-out voices. The students—the convicts—pressed against the blackboard, awaiting execution any time now.

Only the noon meal would suspend the adventures for a little while. The mailman interrupted too. The house was close to the street, across the way from the tall building where he made his stop. He would prop his bicycle against the electric pole. When he came out, his big pouch of worn reddish leather was almost empty. He got on his bike, the wheels turned, the spokes caught the sun.

Starting at ten in the morning, the students came in a steady stream, replacing one another at intervals. They climbed a few steps; the ground floor was above street level. You could hear them wiping their feet for a long time. They knocked on the door, paused, came in shyly: children, real gentlemen, young ladies. Pretty scared, all of them. Very slowly they pulled out books and notebooks. But no matter how long they tried to put it off, they would still end up at the blackboard.

In the first room, the large one, the blackboard occupied the entire left-hand wall. When filled and pushed upward, it would uncover the other one behind it. Scared and hesitant voices were heard from the corner, mixed with the shouts of the executioner.

Gradually, the boy's amazement, enchantment, and fear quieted down. It hadn't been difficult to understand that he wasn't really in a madhouse, only a sort of summer school, when school was on vacation. Preparations for the baccalaureate, the qualifying exams for high school, the makeup exams.

Often it wasn't just one teacher and one student. The principal worked with his students on arithmetic, algebra, trigonometry. His blond wife would whisper at the corner table with another convict: *la prune, la pomme, la poire, l'abricot.* The principal's shouts were muted only when the buzzing of the people at the table swelled. They had just come, of course, to the usual family of names: *la feuille, le feuillage, feuilleter, le feuilleton, le feuilletage.* The principal's sister and brother were also professors of mathematics, with teachers for husbands and wives: of French, history, physics.

From morning to night, the groans, the whimperings, the howlings, the fury, the suffering brought the walls down. At times words would break away, stray from their sources, and float down by the corner of the sofa: *pyramid, pentagon, le professeur, le grand-père, the pendulum, Napoléon, Athena, the laws of the pendulum, Ohm's law, Joule's law, Pythagoras, famille de mots.* The blackboard, white with chalk, was burned by circles and red fractions, pierced by green arrows, until it was transformed by the sponge into elongated yellow and blue festoons.

It hadn't been hard to figure out, down to the hour, the order the students showed up in, from one day and one week to the next, how the teachers followed one another. Except for the boy's shadow curled on the sofa, no one else from the family was allowed into the big front room. Once in a while, the white-haired, arthritic old woman, mother of the math teachers, would come in. She would rinse out the sponges in the bucket; the water turned red, green. She would deposit the soiled sponge next to the blackboard, rise on tiptoes, and apply another sponge. Across the way, gentlemen with briefcases would come out of the gray building, one after the other.

WITH TIME, connections were deduced, symmetries disclosed. A week later, when the mailman got on his bike again and the spokes of the wheels filled one's retina for an instant, in the room you'd find, of course, just like this Saturday—you could bet on it—Emilia, the principal's sister, the one who howled louder than anyone else, and sometimes jumped up, algebra book in hand, ready to throw it at the curls of the young lady with freckles and shrewd, languid eyes. Only such things could bring alive the diagrams, the signs appearing and disappearing on the blackboard. But such incidents were losing some of their mystery; they were becoming stale.

But one Tuesday morning, the thin gentleman whose gold fountain pen was stuck in his coat pocket and whose glasses were almost as small as his eyes failed to show up. The principal became furious waiting for him, and looked at his cousin sunk on the couch. A quiet child, perhaps too frail. Must have fallen behind in many things—who knows. He is wasting time, should be kept busy. Read, reckon, do homework, catch up with his peers. Good idea, of course.

The teachers responded eagerly. They would warm up between tutorials by tossing him back and forth, like a ball. The seven times table, *je suis, tu es, il est,* newspaper articles copied in a large lined notebook . . . Until the day the blond, the principal's wife, took a long look at the boy, saw his pallor, and whispered in her husband's ear. He refused to listen, did not agree, shook his head, and waved her off. Nevertheless, the next day they left him alone, but tolerated him in the room, just as before.

Everything quieted down again, became routine, accepted: no longer amazed, he turned his attention toward the past—without streets or teachers—where no one had heard of Pythagoras, Pericles, and *grand-père;* toward questions about the miracle that had parted the realms; about how long this present one would last; or about who had been left in the abandoned worlds. All this till one Friday, after lunch, the principal chased the boy's thoughts away with a friendly pat on the shoulder:

"I brought you a book of fairy tales."

And on top of it all, he—who was feared even by his own brother and sister—had smiled.

FIRST THERE had been the things to eat, along with their names, then had come the first clothes, with their names too. And now here was the first book of fairy tales, which he was entering, unprepared. . . .

The front room and its scholastic executions were increasingly left behind. He stayed in the bedroom with its many beds and dim light. It's too dark, he's spoiling his eyes, the old woman said. Especially, she added, since he has his eyes glued to the book from morning to night. What's more, in the last two weeks he's had time to read it twenty times over.

The good old woman had now become white as winter, gloomy as bad weather. She took him to the kitchen, where, as agile as a young maiden, she would make lye from ashes in the tub and mix mush with tiny bits of food while from the yard the songs of birds entered through the open door. As if she didn't know what more to do for him to grow handsome, jolly and fat, round like a melon. Sitting at the table, reading the book for the umpteenth time, the boy wouldn't utter a word.

Twenty-five times in twenty-five days he went back to the mud hut where he had lived five or five hundred years before, buried in dirt and darkness, scruffy, mangy, grunting among his kind, until one afternoon, on Holy Friday, he came to grips with the enchantment, the fright of the things he had read.

To verify the magic, he closed the book with its thick covers wrapped in green fabric, set it down, and shut his eyes. Perched quietly on the chair, alone in the house, he blew hard through his nostrils. As anticipated, out came two bursts of flame; he saw a bridge studded with precious stones, trees on both sides where exotic birds sung. As it was written, over lands and seas, through forests and deserts he made his way to the Monastery of Incense, where he lay down on carpets as thick as sofas. When he opened his eyes he could no longer see all the marvels of the palace: the white walls, the opaline ceiling with green edges, the golden rings of the draperies, the tray with the golden hen and chicks, the knightly chairs, the convicts' blackboard, the majestic and soft throne in the corner of the big room.

Then, on Saint Wednesday, Saint Friday, Saint Sunday, the courtiers appeared again, masters of devilry and wizardry, masters of witcheries and tortures, to put the convicts to the test.

Sometimes, through the large windows, you could see the lame heron rushing over the mountains on the old bike. The spokes of the wheels turned fast, swish, swish, the disks would whir on the sidewalk across the street.

The wonder-working principal had really proved that life at the Monastery of Incense was wonderful. And a golden bridge, studded with precious stones, stretched over all that had once been in another realm.

But as darkness descended the spell broke. The daring, handsome youth, now hesitant in his movements, did not dare leave the soft, high throne by himself. Late at night the courtiers carried him to bed. He didn't know what fairy tales meant, but he understood that anything could become anything, like the little pig who rooted through the house during the day and at night shed his hide to turn into the emperor's son.

In the evening he sometimes suffocated on the smell of burned pork rind, his nostrils full of ash and that horrendous stink. It scared him; everything could change in one night, a night five years long—the emperor's son could become what he had just been, with no one to recognize or save him. The fairy tales were real, and each one held a threat. They were real, he felt it, the old story is coming back. The fear had come back.

THE
INSTRUCTOR

HE SPOKE little, his voice more tired than severe. Now and then he frowned; when he did, his gestures took on some animation.

He was on edge. He shifted the blunt pencil stub from one hand to the other, twisting it nervously between his fingers. It was no longer possible to ignore him. Then the bizarre, staccato soundtrack started up: he blew his thick, veined nose repeatedly. His voice came through muffled against a white and foggy background.

His sentences were sometimes spoken with a strange vibrato that meant they shouldn't be taken seriously. At other times he pretended to joke, as if he were avoiding something painful and secret.

"Why is it that the children of the learned are rarely learned? So that it can't be said that learning is hereditary!"

It wasn't the lesson itself so much as the pauses following such diatribes that lengthened the silences between them so horribly. Embarrassment at waiting for something you were in no mood for. In the presence of this odd and shabby teacher, the afternoon's colors slowly faded.

Every day was a whirlwind for the boy. Barely four years had passed since the end of the war. He had been parachuted into a sunny valley; sweet-smelling houses, fat aunts, pathetic old men. His eyes, always alert, had barely been able to withstand the bewilderment. The silky sweet caresses had begun. The tinkling voices of small cousins; the delirium of trays full of pastries; the frolicking with ribbons and beads; cups of milk; soft shiny shoes; ink-stained school benches.

April dust in his nostrils; starched linen, morning, voices, flames, the rainbow, the clatter of promises, the sun blinding you on the swing. He had opened himself entirely and was ready to get started. He had made up the lost classes; devoured textbooks, even those others found dull; he swallowed everything; always hungry, concentrated, impelled by his own thirst.

Later, the first conflicts: the calm and the compromise became oppressive. The looks his family gave him were irritating. His parents transmitted a kind of silent alarm to each other that made them appear shy and ridiculous.

By the second lesson, that fool had clarified his position: "I don't want to waste your time or mine. I can leave, but someone else will come. I knew your grandfather, I know your mother. That's why I've agreed to be here."

The teacher wasn't what he expected. Humbly dressed: a petty functionary, a shopkeeper—the kind that never touches the merchandise—a bored provincial accountant. White hands with burst blood vessels. He was plump, small. His voice was slightly hoarse, his black hat wide-brimmed. Upon his arrival, contrary to the boy's expectations, he had hung it on the coat rack. You had to look very carefully to see the silk skullcap— the color of his bald spot—on his head.

He looked like a neighbor who had dropped by for some unimportant business, let's say to cheer up some invalid. To engage in conversation, give advice, simply to share one of those problems that life delivers unexpectedly. An unknown relative called upon in a difficult moment. But he wasn't a neighbor, he lived who knows where, and he wasn't a relative at all. No, no.

Often inattentive, lost in thought, he would wipe a big white handkerchief over his hot red forehead and its protruding veins. Then he would fold the handkerchief carefully and return it, one corner sticking out, to the pocket below his lapel. The other handkerchief, the one reserved for his nose, the trombone—white too, but gathered in a ball—swelled in the breast pocket of his vest.

The schoolboy he came to see so reluctantly was a sullen partner. His black eyes searched the teacher's for long moments without blinking, but the boy wasn't as rebellious or as insolent as he had expected.

The boy's mother had begged the teacher to try; he was her last hope. The old man had kept his head lowered and did not look at her; as she spoke, he perhaps remembered a dark, slender young woman whose beauty only ten years earlier had made heads turn. This pale woman, bent and always in a panic, seemed much older—she already looked like her mother, who had perished in those cold and disastrous regions from where few had returned. "You know, he's not like the others; for about a year now, it's as if he hated us all. He leaves and doesn't come back until late in the evening, with all kinds of books; he doesn't talk—only a word or two—as if we were a constant imposition. He avoids us, he'd be happier if we didn't exist." Only for her suffering did the teacher reluctantly accept the role.

The first time the man showed up was on a Monday afternoon. It was raining. He did not have an umbrella; wet and shrunken, he had crept along under the eaves. He knocked at the window, as arranged. The boy was home alone. The teacher took off his dripping hat and wet black coat. He was wearing a vest; under the vest, undershirts and sweaters. A small white beard. His pale silk skullcap was barely noticeable. Sharp eyes, pink cheeks freshly shaven. A wide, knotted forehead. He had already buried his thick nose in the handkerchief and was blowing hard, playing for time. "You shouldn't speak to him as to a child, don't attack his new ideas, avoid them; forgive him, he is blind," the mother had most likely advised him. As he sneezed into the handkerchief, the stranger was probably recapitulating everything he knew about the silent young man sitting to his right.

"You're about to turn thirteen, to become a man. That's why I've been called. The ceremony is not complicated. The language is old, beautiful. The greatest book of all was written in it. That is why the language has survived to this day. Precise, like geometry . . . I know you like mathematics. You'll find it interesting."

This old rubbish did not interest the rebellious boy at all. He was sure that he could defend himself against all this, that he could meet head-on whatever clever trap they might lay for him.

"I'll teach you to read it. The pronunciation, the rhythm of the phrases, the tenses. They're complicated. And that will be all, don't worry," continued the guest, folding the handkerchief and stuffing it in the breast pocket of his vest.

He had gotten up and turned toward the coat rack. He picked up a fat brown briefcase that was peeling in places. Where had he kept the briefcase and when had he put it down there?

The teacher picked the case up and rested it against the leg of the table. Bending over, he took out a thick old black tome and a thinner volume that looked like a primer. Then a kind of envelope made out of black cloth that he laid on the table, on top of the books.

"Our men bear witness to their affiliation through two tests. One is permanent and private, and this is done at birth, as you probably know. The second is public, visible. . . ."

From a little black cloth sack he took out two strange bundles. Two small black leather cubes mounted on a somewhat larger square, also made of leather, to which long, thin leather thongs were attached.

"These are placed, one on the left arm, the other on the forehead. The leather comes from an unblemished animal, as the law requires. The arm is bound first. Preference is given to the deed, to action. When we made the covenant, we promised that we would carry out the commandments, and only later would we try to understand them. In observing them we have also learned to grasp their meaning. I hear you know a little philosophy. We are servants of the One whom we have acknowledged and who has chosen us."

Was this a dialogue? He rattled on as long as he pleased. This was no more than static interference on a soundtrack.

"I know this doesn't interest you. Well, let's gloss over the explanations. I thought I'd mention them, as a curiosity. Then the other is put on the forehead. There should be no break between these operations. Nothing to separate the idea from the gesture, the sentiment from the act that inspires and expresses it."

Before leaving, the teacher made sure to show the schoolboy the first pages of the new primer, the strange letters with which he had to become familiar for the next time.

It was getting late; his parents had not returned yet. The stranger gathered his things, wrapped himself up in his still-damp coat, and mumbled something unintelligible as a farewell. Darkness clouded the window. Silence, solitude, absent parents; there was no one to whom to express his contempt for this hour of nonsense.

"They are placed on the left arm, next to the heart, and on the head. A covenant! Of all peoples on earth You chose only me. The people had said: He is ours and He is the only One! I, in turn, grant you uniqueness!"

Now it was night, he was alone. The cold and damp room resounded with the pompous words.

He couldn't forget his parents' pleas, their reproaches over his estrangement and brutality, as if the earth were once again falling into that dark, greenish mire from which they had just emerged. Nor could he forget the nights when the threat of the past came alive with the shiny steel eyes of guns aimed to fire. Nor could he forgive himself that he had finally given in. He was furious that he had been swayed by their insistence and their tears.

A man, he was entering the ranks of men! But he wouldn't let himself be dazzled by incense and old rubbish, nor by stories about his great-grandfather, who at the age of thirteen had married his great-grandmother, aged eleven, nor by sacred leather cords, the skin of unblemished animals, long-winded prayers. And at the end of the ceremony there would be a short speech. Then he would be offered—as between men!—a small glass of brandy, a small piece of cake, stale jokes.

It was only while recollecting their past that he found himself part of his family. For the rest, no bridge remained. After all they had lived through, suddenly he was seeing them from a great distance. They seemed childish, ridiculous. They did not even believe in the ceremony for which they were preparing him. It was just the need for yet another sign that all was normal. Nothing else but the rush to accumulate proof, to have relatives and neighbors and former friends confirm that, yes, everything was in order, that life had reaccepted them, that it was just like *before*, that they were the same as before. All customs had to be properly observed: the spectacle for which they had invited such a learned and benign quack was but one instance of the staged scenes to which they were prepared to submit themselves, hour by hour, day in and day out.

He was a man, the only one among them! His eyes were dilated with fury. A true fighter would have recognized in him, he had no doubt of it, a worthy companion. What a man thinks at thirteen is as important as what he will think at thirty.

Adults, sure of themselves, meted out verdicts, made senseless speeches, told banal anecdotes, repeated endless stories whose thread they had lost. No, flashed the hostile eyes of the implacable and self-important boy, he would not be like them. One weakness, then another, then another: a real man would have avoided such confrontations, he would have demonstrated that he was in control of his powers and of his isolation. In vain he had tried to avoid painful compromises. He thought he was going to die of shame from the botched rebellion, from the crying that did not surface but twisted him inside. He was overcome by dizziness; he wanted air, light, water, a refuge where no one could find him.

He had been holding his jacket in his hand for several minutes. Soon his parents would be back, and there would be an overly cheerful reunion.

Outside it was no longer raining; if he hurried he might still catch the film, or he could wander the streets. He would come back late, when they could no longer ask him anything.

He returned late. In the kitchen he found the tray with bread, butter, a glass of milk. He drank the milk, then carefully pulled out the book hidden under the cupboard.

They were sleeping, or pretending to; it did not matter. They had become used to his extravagances and no longer nagged at him about rules.

He pulled the lamp closer and opened the book. The inflammatory first phrase had repeated its clear black cadence to him many times: "A specter is haunting Europe . . . A specter is haunting Europe." The sound became deafening. "All the Powers of old Europe have entered into a holy alliance to exorcise this specter." The thundering voice filled the entire screen, you could no longer see anything but those burning syllables: "The history of all hitherto existing society is the history of class struggle. . . . The bourgeoisie, wherever it has got the upper hand, has put an end to all feudal, patriarchal, idyllic relations. . . . It has left no other nexus between man and man than naked self-interest. . . . It has drowned the most heavenly ecstasies of religious fervor, of chivalrous enthusiasm, of philistine sentimentalism, in the icy water of egotistical calculation. In a word, for exploitation, veiled by religious and political illusions, it has substituted naked, shameless, direct, brutal exploitation."

On Wednesday the teacher appeared again, punctually, along with the rain. This time he had a huge patched umbrella and a shiny black raincoat closed up to the neck. Quickly, without introduction, he turned to the alphabet and the first words.

They started with grammar: nouns, pronouns, verbs. Ordinary teaching, like geography or history or algebra. The old man did not find it hard to admit that the young man was a good student. The instructor was not stingy with praise; the best, he finally mumbled.

Encouragement before the approaching holidays. A cold, rainy fall, clear days, the end of September, the household strictures. They did not beg him again, as they had a year earlier, to join them under the vast, cold cupolas. They were keeping their word, they did not ask the impossible of him: they did not expect there to be any connection between the lessons of Monday, Wednesday, Thursday, and reality. So they were not serious, they were not consistent.

Thursday's lesson, conjugating irregular verbs—and the verbs of this rigorous language were proving to be mostly irregular.

The lesson ended a little early. The great expert closed his book more quickly than usual. It was over, but it was not. In his chair, his head lowered between his shoulders, he was no longer looking at his student.

"For us, forgiveness is not simply a hypothesis. It has been proved, it has taken place. After forty days of prayer, in place of the destroyed tablets we were given new ones."

His speech was slow, hoarse. He took out the wrinkled white handkerchief from the breast pocket of his black vest but did not use it, as usual, to blow his trumpet of a nose. He held the handkerchief in his fist, on his right knee, next to the leg of the table.

"For us, penance follows rather than precedes judgment. The judgment must remain fair, unswayed. For us, conscience—you understand the word, you probably use it every day—for us, moral judgment is not irreversible."

Concentrating, he did not look up, as if he were whispering only to himself. But, the joker, he still found time for ironies; he had not forgotten his tricks. But the shrewd, respectful distancing of "us" and "you" no longer had the effect it had earlier. The old man knew the weight of words; otherwise he would not have used them with so much difficulty, panting, hoarse, leaving long pauses between them.

"The believer, that is, the learned man, we could call him that, that would suit you better, he must realize that sin does not lead inexorably to divine punishment. Our conscience allows for recuperation; forgiveness is possible."

Evening had descended; it was quiet, and hard to interrupt him. The words emerged slowly. At long intervals they erupted—uncertain and fragile, they seemed to be asking for a prudently warm reception to be able to rise, to make themselves heard.

"At the New Year the righteous are judged according to the strict letter of the law. Only the righteous deserve severity. On the day of forgiveness, during the great fast that follows the New Year, those in the middle, those who are neither like this nor like that—the ordinary ones, the owners of good deeds and bad—are judged with clemency. And the sinners can repent. They too can be forgiven if they change their ways. Misdeed against God, of course! Misdeeds against people must be forgiven by people."

He had grabbed his impeccable handkerchief out of the pocket under the lapel of his jacket and buried his trumpet deep in the white silk square. The other handkerchief was on the corner of the table. At some point he must have opened his fist; the linen ball, the one he used for his large troubled nose, was forgotten. He didn't drag out the process; he simply stuffed the handkerchief back under his lapel.

"Created free, that is, subject to mistakes, we are offered forgiveness by the law itself. Repentance follows, it does not precede, judgment. Judgment must remain above influence, fair. Can true repentance alter the past? Therefore, alter destiny? The future would no longer be a rigorous consequence of past events! Moral judgment is not irreversible. The law permits forgiveness."

Meanwhile he had gotten up slowly, with difficulty. You would have thought he needed a long time to readjust to walking, to the room, to normal movement. But he had quickly put on his hat, his coat, had picked up his briefcase; he had nodded his head and mumbled something, nothing; he opened the door, went into the hall, and was gone.

The house was empty on holidays. Something austerely festive would hover around the freshly dusted walls. The clean room was deserted, cold, mysterious. His parents were away, in that world to which the rebel no longer went. Beneath the high chandeliers of the golden cupola, between the narrow old benches, among other outcasts, hidden by the long white shawls of silk, they were murmuring, swaying to the refrain of the prayers, bending, with abandon, to the ground—the fury of their humiliation transformed into vanity and defiance.

Solitude, quiet—but it was impossible to think. He felt uneasy in that suddenly huge and empty room, where the old man's words still hovered.

"These are the most important days for us. Forgiveness is not simply a hope—it has been granted. Only the righteous deserve a severe judgment. Sin does not lead implacably to punishment. Forgiveness is possible, but only for misdeeds against God. Those committed against men must be forgiven by men. Forgiveness is not quite an absolution. The new tablets were given to the sons of those who had worshiped the golden calf. That is, for their descendants, penitent and forgiven. The second edition was not as great, however. Moral time can be recuperated. Forgiveness is possible, it has been proved. But forgiveness does not absolve! In the Ark, next to the new law, we preserve the shards of the first tablets."

He would have preferred his parents to be there to share that silence. He would have shamed them with his muteness and disapproval as punishment for their timid guilt!

The table covered with velvet, the closed cupboards wiped clean of dust. Sparkling windows, fresh curtains. It could have been pleasant, cozy, yet it was only ambiguous, tortuous.

He rushed to the vacant lot, among the noisy and tough neighborhood boys. He returned late, sweaty, worn out by the running. At the door Lică greeted him with a tasteless joke. The house was still lighted: candlesticks were burning, the white tablecloth shone. His parents, elegant, stiff, avoided looking into each other's eyes. It was as if they did not even see the dirty, cynical wanderer in the doorway.

Just what year had begun *for them*, only folklorists of Near Eastern antiquity or those who read coffee grounds could have known. But honored parishioners, it *is* October 1! You know that very well because yesterday you got paid. The year did not follow nebulous and sanctified legends; the year was coming to an end . . . winter was coming, but not according to *your* lunar calendar, in which the oxen still pulled a wooden plow.

Instruction continued, however, in the exercise of divine linguistics. The verbs, adverbs, nouns multiplied. Outside, it was snowing thick and fast on the newer, dissident religions.

THE LESSONS continued rigorously. Gone were the pathetic theological digressions, but now came the rules: grammar, vocabulary, translation, composition. An agreement of limited participation. Again Monday, Wednesday, Thursday, conjugations, declensions, adjectives, numerals, attributives, complements, predicates, vocabulary, translation, composition. The black coat on a hook, the black hat on a hook, the briefcase next to the coat rack, the crumpled handkerchief to blow in, the white formal handkerchief. The short, stocky middle-aged gentleman—who could have been from the tax office or the forestry services or from nowhere at all, a court clerk, a tailor, a doctor's assistant, a violinist, a cashier, a detective: a conscientious, laconic scholar, within the limits of the contract.

The schoolboy discovered late and by accident that after the end of the lesson a film, a popular short catering to the tastes of the masses, was screened in the kitchen. The boy was just going there to get a drink of water when he caught the hoarse voice of the speaker. He retreated into the sepia shadows. "Saturday morning on his way to prayers, the rabbi from

Berdichev met the town rebel. To confront the rabbi publicly, the rebel took out his pipe and lighted it. The rabbi stopped before the sinner. You must have forgotten that today is Saturday. No, I haven't forgotten at all, the rebel replies insolently. Then you probably don't know that we are not allowed to smoke on Saturday. Not at all! I know all your laws, replies the rebel. The rabbi from Berdichev does not allow himself to be provoked. Then he raises his eyes and speaks to the sky: Did you hear? He's challenging your commandments. But you have to admit: no one can make him lie! That was the rabbi from Berdichev, kindness incarnate. He saw only good. . . . But after taking a few steps, he turned again toward the boor, who remained standing in the street in confusion. Why are you doing this? Because I'm an atheist! said the rebel, puffing himself up. So you're an atheist, mumbles the rabbi from Berdichev thoughtfully. Aha, hmm. And at which yeshiva and with whom did you study? What do you mean, yeshiva, what kind of yeshiva? stammered the rebel. Well, after all, you can't be an atheist unless you study the holy books. That was the rabbi from Berdichev, wisdom incarnate."

An allusion? Is he in fact speaking about the sinner he's now teaching? Is he kindness incarnate? So, the uninvited guest also poked fun at his student after souring three of his afternoons a week with moldy fruit.

The film droned on lazily. The merchant of anecdotes and soporifics continued with the same generous narratives:

"One day a young man comes to see the rabbi: I've been married for several years, I don't have any issue, I'm desperate, my wife and I want to have children. All right, says the rabbi from Berdichev, go home, you'll have a child. Nine months later, the young man returns, joyous: a son is born. Soon afterward, another solicitant comes to see him: I want a child, I've been married for five years, help me. He receives the same answer: go home, you'll have a child. A month passes, another two go by, another two, the promise is not fulfilled."

As the boy listens, the floor squeaks; it is a narrow space filled with baskets, bags, pots, only a step to the tiny, pantry-sized kitchen with its open door. You need the skills of a tightrope walker to stand there and not make the floor creak beneath your feet.

"The young man returns furious and embittered: You promised and it has not come true, I'm in despair. The old man shrugs his shoulders: What can I do? For you it was impossible. The wretched man insists, shouting: Why not for me? Why was it possible for the other? Because the other, after he left me, went straight to the store and bought a baby carriage! What did you do? the old man asked him. I don't know, I don't remember, stammered the blockhead. Well, that's why . . . that was why it wasn't possible, the rabbi sighed sadly. That was the rabbi from Berdichev, faith incarnate."

The weeks went by. Monday, Wednesday, Thursday: declensions, conjugations, translation, composition. "The rabbi from Berdichev said: Once I saw a thief the moment they caught him. I heard him murmuring: Tomorrow I'll have another go at it, I'll be better next time. The thief taught me that you have to start again every day." Again Monday, Wednesday, Thursday, the hat on the hook, the handkerchief, a-choo, grammar, vocabulary, translation. "The rabbi from Kotsk used to say: Prayers in hell are more sincere than those in heaven. That was the gloomy rabbi from Kotsk. He would shout: I prefer a dyed-in-the-wool idol worshiper to a half-believer! His last words: At last I'll see Him! Face to face!"

Another week: verbs, adverbs, prepositions, conjugations.

"Every nation can be understood by its language and grammar. Look at the English, dignified and democratic: both the king and the garbage man write 'I' with a capital letter. And we . . . for us there is no formal 'you.' We call everyone by his first name, and we all have a direct connection with God, without intermediaries."

Again, the coat, hat, briefcase, handkerchief, notebooks full of rules and signs, the stop in the kitchen; the lady of the house offers him a cup of coffee: "The rabbi from Berdichev, the kindest of men, once broke off in the middle of his Yom Kippur prayers. He looked up and shouted, 'Today we are all prostrated before You, waiting for Your judgment. But I say, *You* shall be judged by all who suffer and die to sanctify Your name, Your laws, and Your contracts!' On another occasion, he murmured, 'I am not asking You why we are persecuted and massacred everywhere and under any pretext, but I would like to know at least if we are suffering for You.'

"And the rabbi from Kotsk struck his fist against the table and roared, 'I require that justice be carried out! That the Supreme Legislator subject himself to his own laws!' "

THE ICE on the eaves was melting; the girls had reappeared, and with them their heady spring scent. The vacant lots roared with big soccer matches; in the morning and at dusk spring vertigo intoxicated the youth, who whirled around and around, poisoned by exotic breezes. Drunken roosters, conceited dogs, and music-crazed cats danced around the fences to the syncopated rhythm of madness.

A documentary of the times recording its events, burdens, and problems would register that on Monday, Wednesday, Thursday there was nothing but old parchments and scrolls: spring was not discussed, nor the international labor day, which was going to be celebrated the following Thursday, nor what had happened during the war or at school, nor the passionate films about the days of doubt and triumph. All this was dust for future archives.

The stranger seemed beaten, tired; he no longer jumped out

of his chair, blurting words. The phrases rolled out evenly, in a steady tone, as if from an automaton. He didn't feel the urge to attack, to wait for a reply. He satisfied himself with a modest indifference. Sunken cheeks, watery eyes. He sweated a lot, panted. His large irritated nose with its wide purplish nostrils troubled him constantly. He blew with gusto into the handkerchief the size of a napkin, then crumpled it up and slipped it hurriedly into the breast pocket of his heavy gray winter jacket, which was buttoned over his vest and woolen sweater, which covered his shirt, which was held tightly closed at the neck by the big knot of his tie.

He had lost the fight. He should have understood long ago that his tricks served no purpose. Perhaps he was sick.

AT THE end of May, the selection of candidates for the summer camp would be announced at school. Everybody was excited by this prospect.

Whether by coincidence or not, just then, when no one would have expected it anymore, the psalmist recovered his taste for chatter, the courage of familiarity. Again he was playing the part of an old relative passing through town and happy to exchange a word or two, to allow a joke or a piece of advice to slip out, just like that, by accident. Thoughts, anecdotes, questions, pleasantries, it soon became clear that, in fact, they were perfidious attacks! That's what was decided by the boy and Lică during their dialectical discussions. Cunning and perfidiousness: there was no other way to explain why the great actor had returned to tricks that had proved useless.

"Let's call it learning, not faith. You who are thirsty, seek water! That is one of our sayings."

The appeal was no more than a hidden trap from which thin, curved, poison-tipped arrows whizzed out.

"Faith exists where it is allowed to gain admittance. You too have allowed faith to enter. Even if it is not the right one."

And further, after a resumption of conjugations, declensions, translations:

"Do you know what we say? Even if it goes in one ear and out the other, still a trace is left along the way. Too young? A temporary defect! You're losing this disability with every passing day."

Finally, before putting the black bowl over his bald spot, he would push the pedal *"you—us,"* which he had taken up again with fervor.

"When all is said and done, beliefs aren't all that different. I see that you have saints. But we don't have them! Saints, no, we don't have that. No man is so righteous that he can be good without sinning. There are wise men, naturally. So we had better call it learning, that will suit you too."

Look where it gets you: you make one concession, then another, until bang, the stranger slaps you in the face. You did not hit back in time; he knows that now you can't! You can't anymore.

Now he knew that something had changed: for the moment the rebel's hands were tied; anything could be done to him. His parents had found out about the camp. A fine bargaining chip had been offered them. They were suddenly in control and could use it without scruples: in the event you are chosen, if you want to have our consent, you'll have to be kind to Mr. Teacher Accordionist Carpenter Detective, whatever he might be, for all the nonsense he has had the goodness to share with you in between sneezes every Monday, Wednesday, Thursday, his eminence, our very hoarse benefactor.

The instructor had been informed about the blackmail; there was no other explanation for the oblique, increasingly cutting familiarities.

"Every beginning is dizzying. And happiness? As if that were anything. . . . Suffering, only suffering gives weight to time! Write this down, you can write down anything you want, I know who you are, the company you keep. I know you feel guilty that you're here listening to this old-fashioned idiot. Guilt can be vengeful, I am used to it. I hear you appear on the podium for celebrations. You hold conferences, you recite, maybe you also write poems, the red kind. Write it down, write it down, I'm not afraid."

The sequence accelerates in rhythm with the chatter. "The verses written on parchment speak of love, reward, punishment. The truth, in other words. And about freedom. Do you know of anything more important than these delusions? You consider man guilty. You always suspect him. But do you think *we* don't? We say: You have been born, therefore you are guilty."

Shooting was becoming difficult; the camera turned toward the window, then the sky and the trees in the yard.

"Unanimity? Every man is unique, not only God! In the old days our highest court very rarely condemned anyone to death. Only for truly extraordinary crimes! Even then, however, the people did not praise their judges for that. But there existed a provision that automatically annulled the death sentence: if the sentence was passed unanimously. It's suspicious, comrade, what can I say. Are you taking notes? Look at that, maybe you're interested. Do you want to turn me over to the Inquisition? There have been many cases, it wouldn't be the first time. Write it down, son, write this down too: 'The wise man in fur.' A man shielded from the cold feels free to think he's smart. For you people, it's not even a matter of wise men. You have saints. In fur."

What is one supposed to make of that? Sunday morning, in the laziness of the colorless hours, the candidate tries to inject

surprise by officially announcing the summer event to the con-
spirators. Extraordinary scene! Wide eyes, happiness, kisses, as
if they hadn't known anything about it. They seem sincere: the
head of the family rushes out to buy a bottle of wine; the lady
of the house runs over to the neighbors' with the news. Such
perfect acting, spontaneous, without the faintest sign of hostility
or deviousness. One is almost ready to believe them. No question of opposing the trip, they were proud, happy. Try to
understand what is going on now! Such cunning seemed to be
too much for their warm hearts. And yet no, no, one had to
keep one's eyes open; no detail should be ignored.

There was no longer any doubt—the small, apparently inof-
fensive, perspiring, hoarse man was hiding behind his innocent
game and inexpressive mask; he was an expert schemer! The
parents' pained tenderness and his otherworldly geniality were
no more than modulations in falsetto. The playful or aggressive
words, the high didactic professionalism, hid more than they
disclosed. The pedagogue was their powerful secret weapon.

When it was lesson time the house suddenly became quiet.
This was unusual. Nothing ever interrupted the continuous
circulation from the kitchen into the room, from the room into
the hall. Slammed doors, chatter, relatives, neighbors, friends,
white-collar workers, Martians, Neanderthals, there was constant turbulence. The appearance of old what's-his-name,
however, instantly stopped the merest sound, the slightest
movement.

In the room, the grammarian goes hoarse with his anachro-
nistic phonetics. Not a word is to be heard, there isn't even a
breeze from the yard. Even if eyes and ears are spying, the
doors seem securely locked, the rooms empty; the walls, suddenly thick and porous, absorb all noise. The soundtrack starts
suddenly; the movements take on speed.

"You say to deceive your fellow man is a sin. Our elders say to deceive God is childish. Of course. But to deceive yourself, in whom both man and God reside? Be careful, be careful of this."

He kept it up that way, excited, aggressive. When he wanted to focus on a special point that he did not have the courage to express outright, he would modulate his voice dramatically or gesticulate rapidly as though ready to grab his adversary by the shoulders and shake him. "Pay attention, pay attention to this." One did not know what to expect from his commotion. The old man allowed himself to be transported to the point of frenzy by the onrush of his delirium.

Bizarre ideas, not at all innocent. "You can take notes, go ahead, write it down." He knows that it is easier to keep calm when taking notes, like an automaton, than to have to listen.

The parents had pinned all their hopes on the instructor. A few seconds before his arrival they would disappear, vanish, as if they didn't dare disturb his mission. Or perhaps they felt some guilt toward him; it couldn't be ruled out. Was guilt the mysterious element in their relationship? Was their guilt—the boy's guilt—the explanation behind their obvious subordination? One week he didn't show up. Because of illness, that's what they said. They became helpless, stumped, as if life had lost its focus.

Like a miracle, a bizarre compensation, rumors of a polio epidemic suddenly seized their attention. The disease was spreading quickly in this district or that, in this boarding school or that.

Disarmed, barely hiding their panic, each day his parents brought fresh disturbing news. So-and-so from this village, that village. So many in this city or that. Special care should be taken by those who had been through the difficult years, those weakened by fear, by hunger. The undernourished, fussy, sensitive, weak children. Particularly vulnerable were those who had suffered in the war! They say that a tailor's daughter who had been in the same concentration camp with us . . . Crowded places, poor sanitation, should be avoided. Movie theaters, swimming pools, summer camps were particularly disastrous, because all kinds of people from all over the place come together. The trains too, of course—especially when you've got a long trip ahead of you, a very long trip. They emphasized this information with obvious conviction.

They would unfold the map and pore over the train schedule, looking for Radna. From there a bus would take the Pioneer leaders, the school political guardians, to the castle. At camp the danger would be increased; the risk was catastrophic. As if their wailing and exaggeration could have upset anyone! They laid their traps, made insinuations, threats, gave advice, and then waited for the effect.

The old man reappeared, his thoughts elsewhere. Who could guess why. The rehearsals accelerated, but he did not exert himself; he only repeated summary instructions about the text and acted out stage movements.

"They are placed on the left arm, next to the heart, and on the head. Every day for morning prayer, except for Saturdays and holidays." When he left, the big black hat covered him completely, like a sort of umbrella.

On his last day, during the dress rehearsal, the instructor remained silent, apathetic for half an hour, as if he were hiding in his own shell. One might give in to pity if one wasn't careful! One could have believed that the man was someone else entirely! We do not know whom to admire, Maestro: the famous folklorist, well known in academic forums, as the myopic mathematician who sits in the second row insists; the former advocate for the poor, the scandal of the community, as Lică the know-it-all cousin believes; or the secret philanthropist peddling wisdom and sneezes. He was a kind of legend, or so he seemed with his one and only heavy black suit, in full summer, as if nothing could touch or move him.

But the cold, cough, and sneezing would not stop, no matter how untouchable he believed himself to be. He continued to sit in silence and frown in the direction of the star of the performance.

But surprise! He began to speak, quietly and with difficulty, almost in a whisper, looking straight at his listener. They were nonsense words without the least connection to the immediate and glorious duties of the actor whom he had trained with so much patience, nor to the glorious past that some said he embodied.

"Our magnificent contribution, and ours alone, is this sacred and venerable day, its royal majesty, the Sabbath! We were the first to introduce rest, a symbol of freedom and rebirth!"

Gradually he had raised his voice; he would have shouted had his hoarseness allowed it.

"And of dignity, sir! The symbol of creation! After six days the Lord rested, as we do too. We gave the idea to the world, mind you! And the Holy Book is divided into fifty-four chapters, that's how many joys there are in a year, comrade!"

Then why did you talk to the peasants about cooperatives and phalansteries, why did you defend the atheists and rebels, why did you argue with my grandfather in the temple only to save him later from that horrible trap laid for him . . . and why do you continue to respect an outdated tradition, all these ridiculous customs inherited like a weight, from our ancestors . . .

There hadn't been time for these questions: the hat, coat, and handkerchief had disappeared. He had left. Brusquely, without a word.

The next day, beneath the tall chandeliers, the film became festively colored. A hushed cool hall, the strange smell of old, unfamiliar plants. No one but the boy's father, standing a step behind him, saw his momentary hesitation before he touched the scrolls. The left arm covered, the forehead held tightly in the circle of leather, the black cube in the center. A tense and pale candidate under the sacred white silk shawl in which they had wrapped him. The speech had been perfect, the diction clear. The actor's father, a true gentleman, impeccably dressed, had emerged suddenly, or so it seemed, from his secondary role. And his mother was crying, naturally, as was the rest of the vulnerable and emotional audience.

The instructor had not come to the ceremony. His oddness justified any assumption. Lică had come up with a new invention: he claimed the old man had recently insulted a Party boss, a man he had once defended in court when the Communist Party had been illegal. Moreover he was said to have done so in public. In the process he had alienated everyone and managed to have himself disbarred. He was now thrust into poverty, rejected, ridiculed. If this was true, all the more reason why ceremonies might annoy him, Lică explained from under his extraordinary new mustache. His mission had in fact ended, continued Lică, and there would be no reason for the man to expect final thanks from this spoiled Pioneer.

The epilogue—with brandy, congratulations, and sweet pastry—did not last long. On the street the young man again confronted the lazy, torrid indifference of summer. The burning pavement sank under his steps; the heat melted the solemnity of the day.

A week later the early-morning train started for Radna, at the other end of the country. A long journey with many stops to pick up other Pioneer leaders along the way.

A day and a night on dusty wooden benches. In every district another hero climbed aboard; each a fighter who had proved that he had excelled at his brave and important mission. This was the first international summer camp, with special guests. The boy arrived exhausted: he had thrown up constantly.

They were transported, crowded on top of their suitcases, in a truck from the station to the edge of the forest. A blue sky, white puffs of dandelions, a round sun, fields and hills, a marvel. Although they were tired, they sang; they were happy, proud to represent their country.

At the edge of the wood, twenty Bulgarian Pioneers were lined up waiting for them. They were in uniform; their ties were skinnier, shinier. On their heads they wore white cloth hats that looked like pith helmets.

The scene is colored in summer hues, a panoramic image: the road, the trees, the camp housed in the castle of a former ruling monkey. Flags, trumpets, files of men, gatherings, games, meetings. In the morning, exercises, in the evening, campfires, speeches.

They are preparing for elections; there is a lot of commotion around a stalwart, handsome, brown-haired boy; the children whisper that he is from the capital.

Only a few days after the elections are over do copies of the Pioneer magazine arrive. The boy picks one up, overwhelmed, bashful, proud. The title on the second page sparkles, emphatic and red. Two whole columns! He hides the copy so that no one may catch him looking at it; he does and does not want to be discovered. He becomes friends with a Bulgarian Pioneer leader; they exchange stamps. The boy reveals his secret, and soon word is out; his torment ends.

Naturally his prestige grows. Everyone wants to know everything about him; envious, they barrage him with questions. The instructors introduce him all around. They look at him with interest, ask him questions on everything, nod approval, smile. The next day at roll call they raise their hands to greet him. He does make friends with one of them, a student at the film institute. He looks like a movie star. Slim, cold blue eyes, a Greek profile, the shoulders of an athlete, windblown hair. He is very cultivated, carries on long discussions about Engels's *Anti-Dühring* and Rolland's *The Soul Enchanted*. But also about books unfamiliar to the boy. In deep thought, the young man talks about his life to his friend, the instructor, under a shady tree. How, freed from the camps, they still stayed over there for almost a year, how he had then started school, had even had time to become a Soviet Pioneer Scout. The student is amazed and repeats the story to the others. In the next few days the director and the head instructor ask him for details; even the cook develops a soft spot for him. The director expresses his regret that he hadn't known all these things before the elections. A popular hero, a cultural authority! At the first campfire meeting he recites his sonorous verses to peace.

Always busy, happy, he has no time to unpack his suitcase. Only later does he discover, hidden at the bottom among the towels, a red silk pouch. He closes the case quickly so that he won't be seen; he turns the key in fury. He is not going to touch those objects, it is all over—he isn't going to continue with the masquerade! He should have thrown it out immediately, the pouch containing those bewitched leather thongs—or, better, have burned it, if he had had the courage. He would do it in the next few days. But he puts it off; he does not find the right moment. He is never alone. He also postpones writing the letter that would inform them of the definitive break. In the dormitory and at roll call and at mealtimes he cannot manage to be by himself; there is always someone who is looking for him. But he had made sure to hide the silk pouch at the bottom of his suitcase, covered with handkerchiefs and socks, stuffed beneath his underwear. He keeps feeling for the key in his pocket.

The following week, the reel is changed; the pace quickens, an uproar, an episode with parents and doctors. On the evening before an official inspection prompted by rumors of polio, fresh sheets and blankets are brought in. A great bustle: beds are moved so there will be fewer per dormitory. Windows are washed, floors scrubbed with turpentine. Lights-out is sounded late. The night sequence: moon and pine trees—the panorama facing the dormitory, where the little men cannot sleep because of their agitation and the smell of turpentine. The night swallows movement, but you can still hear voices; trucks unload cases of bottles and boxes of vegetables. The noise ends only toward morning.

At dawn everyone is dizzy; morning exercises do not take place. The yard is filled with stacks of cases, mineral water, all kinds of boxes and packages. At roll call it is announced that the camp will receive an important visit. The truth was that they all felt wonderful, even though they had drunk water from the tap. Too many in the dormitory? No one minded—there were happy, friendly scuffles. It was not quite clear what the guests wanted to hear; after all, everything had been terrific; they were all happy.

The delegation appears at noon: a fantastic meal. But the mineral water has a funny taste—it stings your tongue. The young man is placed next to a doctor, on the other side of whom sits a woman who is enraged and silent. The boy is being interviewed and gives all the appropriate answers: the sheets are changed regularly, we wash our hands six times a day, we are eight to a dormitory room, we drink bottled water, the food is like this, exercise is like that, everything is as it should be. The delegates seem satisfied; they consult among themselves, go for a walk in the woods once more, and in the evening they leave. After dinner, his friend the instructor slaps him on the shoulder merrily: "Bravo, you're a man I can trust. You can help me with a job."

The next day the young writer becomes his assistant. They

lock themselves in a room in the afternoon and work until late.

At the end of the week, two long-haired fellows with heavy filming equipment on their shoulders come from Bucharest. His instructor friend had probably suggested that he be used in the film. He does not complain; carefully he makes a selection of verses for the Saturday-night campfire, a homage to the beloved Iosif Vissarionovich.

The lens focuses on the field, the moon, the straight black pines, the silent audience of centuries. The night smells of pine needles. The instructor puts his arm around his protégé: a close-up of their faces, then the two continue on their walk through the woods.

"There's no point in going back to yesterday's discussion. You're an intelligent, fair-minded boy; of course, the memories have become deeply ingrained for some of the war's children, it is only natural. But this has no connection with . . ."

"That's exactly what I was saying, too: this cannot have any connection. Then why is it necessary to . . . After all, we're happy here, it's wonderful. Why should we control . . ."

"Oh, here we go again. Congratulations on your verses. You have a way with words, Maestro! Where did you ever pick up words like 'cabalistic' or 'heresies,' what were you saying there, terrestrial, a terrestrial calendar, for everyone. We don't have saints, either naked or covered in furs. Good, comrade, that's right. Her Majesty the Light . . . nice! . . . severity is only for the righteous . . . we believe in you, just as you believe in us . . . Son, you're a man of culture! All right, I'll stop, I understand. Look, you've got a letter."

He hands him the envelope. His father's beautiful, elegant writing. The boy looks at it for a long time and hesitates. The instructor can no longer restrain himself—he begins to laugh.

"I haven't opened it, for God's sake."

He kept laughing—he could not stop. He had gone on

ahead, laughing with unpleasant heartiness. The boy stops, pale. He does not open the envelope; with a frown he watches the departing figure of his companion. The unopened letter, was it an exception? If so, yet another reason for starting the discussion again! Surely, each would repeat his argument and fail to convince the other, not even make him understand. It would end with the same patronizing pat on the shoulder. A man shouldn't get upset. Between friends there should be no room for condescension. But when seriousness is taken for childishness . . . The instructor used any pretext to avoid real talk; he put up a sort of soft wall between them.

In fact it would have been very annoying had the instructor read the letter. *I hope you did not get angry about what you found in the suitcase. I know you are not going to use them. But Mother insisted. We hear all kinds of rumors about polio. She thinks that these things might protect you.*

The concerned tone and careful words did not alter the boy's decision to send a letter announcing his separation from the family. He had a lot to do—he was almost never alone, that was true. But now everything became more difficult. Had the instructor really not opened the letter? Does this mean he wouldn't open the reply? What about the answer: to write it, not to write it?

He had objected to the reading of letters from the very beginning. The panic and the rumors of an epidemic had worried some parents so much that they had not only registered official complaints but had also alarmed the children about it; some had even come all the way to the camp to convince themselves that all was well. This was not, the boy maintained, a sufficient motive for the snooping. In fact, what difference would it make if the letters . . .

He had objected, but he had consented. He too would have to subject himself to the general rule. "I should have written the letter. And in the most categorical of terms. And put it in with all the envelopes ready to be checked."

He couldn't write about the strange objects hidden in his suitcase. He would have had to explain, at least to the instructor, what it was all about.

He was angry to be connected once more to the shadows from which he was now estranged. Yes, he was sure he was estranged. He had taken another road, it was clearly another road. And yet he felt guilt and shame.

He avoided looking at the others, became taciturn. Sometimes he felt nauseated; perhaps he also had a fever. His friend the instructor was kind and concerned, and asked him repeatedly whether he was sick. He was giving him a chance to open up.

The boy hesitated before speaking: "I can't look my roommates in the eye—I know what is in their letters. Not even at the other campers sometimes. For example, the handsome boy from Bucharest who was elected commander. Now I know how much he despises the rest of us, what he wrote about the showers, about the food." The soundtrack came to a stop suddenly, like a sob. The mentor was smiling. He stretched a powerful, tanned hand across the table and squeezed the boy's small and shaking one.

"Forget these things, there's no point. Don't torture yourself anymore. It's my mistake. I shouldn't have involved you in this. After all, you told me about those fears and sufferings. I should have realized. All right, starting tomorrow, you don't have to come anymore."

But the young dreamer returned on the next day, and on the following days, after lunch, at the usual hour, in the narrow office with the naked walls, a table and two chairs. The instructor did not send him away. It was a friendly gesture, gentle and indulgent, toward a dreamy, fragile artist. They worked in silence and left together for their dormitories. The boy can't fall asleep. Outside the window in the night he sees the fiery eyes of a nameless bird.

Only a few days before leaving, he managed to draft a letter. He was in the infirmary, where he had been put for observation: he complained of headaches, nausea, that his legs weren't steady, that he couldn't sleep. They gave him all kinds of pills. Finally he slept. Still he was pale, taciturn, his eyes shone, as though blinded by a strange flame.

> I understand you are worried about polio. There are no cases here, but there is cause for concern. The sheets were changed only when they came for inspection. Then they gave us good things to eat; we drank bottled water. Now they even forget to boil it. We don't wash much. We are fine in the dormitory, though there are many of us. It's crowded in the showers. The doctor hasn't been here in a week. The nurse has no patience; she just got engaged. But I hope to get out of here in one piece.

He knew these lines would punish his parents, the censor, and the rebellious writer himself. He asked the nurse to put the letter in the mailbox by the director's office. From the window he carefully followed the blond as she went to lunch. He saw her drop the envelope into the mailbox.

That same evening they allowed him to leave the infirmary. In the dormitory, he pulled out the suitcase from under his bed. It was untouched, dusty, the way he had left it. He unlocked it. Raising the lid only a fraction, he put in his hand and felt around. Everything was in place.

There was only one day of camp left. That afternoon he did not go to meet his companion. In the evening, a pleasant surprise. Those strong guys, the cameramen, had returned with the film.

At the canteen the film was screened. Morning exercise, roll call, model airplanes, craft classes, dance classes, the campfire, the entertainment programs, meals, excursions, the dormitories, the showers, the volleyball field. Our boy/actor shared the leading role with the commander from Bucharest. He was on the screen for almost two minutes: with the trumpet, at the shower, at the reading, with the flag, next to the Bulgarian boy.

When the lights were turned on, they all clapped. The instructor waved but did not come near him.

The next day, the camp closed in a festive atmosphere. At noon the groups were taken to the station.

The trip back seemed even longer. Heat, crowding. He kept throwing up. There seemed to be endless stops; he did not have the strength to squeeze the hands of those getting off. He would doze for a while, wake up suddenly in a sweat, struggle to reach the toilet and vomit. He had not been able to take out the red silk pouch; he was never alone.

Finally, just before arriving home, he fell asleep. At times, the long silver snout of a phosphorescent shark shone in the black window.

He woke up at the station. Through the window he saw them waiting nervously and impatiently. He was the only one left in the compartment. He still had time to open the suitcase and pull out the pouch. He felt the cube, the leather thongs, and the rustle of the shawl. His hand shook holding that hidden explosive. A frightening, dangerous contact. Furious, he threw the bundle under the seat.

He got off the train, relieved and suddenly cheerful. He told them that everything had been as wonderful as in a fairy tale. They made no comment. Had they received the letter? No one brought it up. He told them about his Bulgarian friend, with whom he planned to exchange letters and stamps. At home he unpacked in front of them. Not a word about the missing object.

They were pleased that the holiday had been such fun. But

they seemed tentative. He told them about the upcoming cinematographic event of which he was the star. They seemed truly moved.

But the anticipated film arrived only months later: fall had settled in over the little town, hunched under sleet and nocturnal winds. A time of rapid growth, of sleeplessness among his books in his cell.

In the belly of the clouds, unseen birds shrieked in the twilight. The little provincial town swayed languidly. In the evening the hills, intoxicated by resin, rolled recklessly toward the mouth of the devil; on the burning roofs, cats and billy goats danced on pyres. The young man takes rigorous walks under the town hall clock, his eyes toward the stars. Aloof, contemptuous, without illusions, proprietor of solitude, keeping step to the rhythm of a number of grand phrases. To deceive the Lord is childish. . . . To deceive your fellow man is a sin. . . . Error above, error below.

Proud, distant, like any beginner; each step marked yet another start. Poor: without error above, without error below. He avoided crowds, skirted market squares, stadiums. He kept away from assembly halls, churches, movie theaters. He stoically bore his poverty, wounds, grandeur, old age, which had come—who would have believed it—so quickly. Look, in only two months. Everything changed, his gait, his voice, smile, vision. He listened to music until late in the night: records, records, until he lost himself in a faint. In the melodic waters of dawn resounded the flap of long metallic wings.

Yet even in the depths of melancholy he would have to watch that childish documentary about the country's first summer camp. He went to the movie theater; it was a Wednesday, around ten in the morning. He realized how judicious his choice had been: at that hour people were at work or at school. The few spectators, wanderers of no importance, did not de-

serve his attention; their curiosity could be ignored. He picked
a spot as far away as possible from anyone.

The program merited no more than condescension. What
could a short, ten-minute film show? A castle, a forest, a troop
of pleasant-looking little schoolboys! The tall entrance gate, the
flags, the volleyball games, the field trip, the campfire, the roll
call, the swimming pool. Everything staged, stylized; they
would omit the nurse, the showers, the narrow censor's office,
and the beautiful secret hiding places in the field. The hero
would appear, probably, in two illustrious, banal sequences, to
touch soft-hearted souls with his idiotic, childish smile.

The clock showed one minute past the hour. A few more
seconds. . . . He closed his eyes; on his inner screen images of
the sky and of the town. A different film: a broken-up street, an
old building, a tapering roof; an ordinary room, a table, a chair,
another chair, at which sits a schoolboy hunched over books
and notebooks. He writes, draws rapidly, or he sits there, perplexed, with an absent look. Another scene: the face of an old
man, a bird, a tiger's snout, the barbed-wire fence. He takes
notes feverishly: the instructor, tousled hair, handkerchief,
Mother, rolls of parchment, a gaunt vulture, the scaly tail, the
black hat; the castle, the tiger, the flags, the spiral horn, the
bird. He mumbles constantly as he writes. Now all that is left
is the pallor of a frowning boy with big eyes. Again, he mumbles as he looks at his drawing: you're here on the page, where
are you always flying to . . . stuck for good, he writes down
another word, draws, takes notes. It is not quite clear what he
is doing and what he is saying; he seems caught up in the
mission that has been entrusted to him. Suddenly he looks at
his watch and rushes to the coat closet. He takes out his beret,
his coat. He slams the front door behind him. Outside, a damp
fall, the streets are dirty, slippery. He walks to the front of a
narrow building, stops at the box office window, goes into a

hall, and sits in the back, on the right, near the exit.

Now the real film starts. Green hills, summer, a castle. Truckloads of schoolboys, flags. Roll call, the volleyball field, the campfire. Roll call, the forest, the infirmary, the games. Next to the flag, under the flag . . . reciting in front of the fire, in the field. A shy, photogenic smile.

The bored spectator gets up. He stops at the snack bar, buys himself a chocolate bar and some juice, and leaves hurriedly.

Out in the street he buries his face in his collar. He heads for the high school, absorbed in his thoughts. In the air, unseen, a gaunt bird, a flame. He touches his temples, his brow. Suddenly he hears the hoarse words of a stranger.

"What are you doing here, young man?"

With a frown he looks up. He can't stand such familiarity. The man is standing before him, a gentleman of medium height in a black coat and hat. A plump, sagging face, deep circles around the eyes, a white, neglected beard.

"Don't you recognize me anymore?"

They are standing under the eaves of a repair shop, protected from the damp wind that is lifting whirlwinds of bronze-colored leaves around them. The young man allows himself a moment's hesitation.

"It's possible that we know each other. This very summer I had, I believe, interesting discussions with you, dear instructor, about Mr. Dühring and about a novel by Romain Rolland. If I'm not mistaken, we even debated certain problems we had come across during our censors' work. You know, without telling you I took the liberty of taking some unsuitable letters. In the evening, before falling asleep, I would reread the delicious childish confessions, full of candor and cunning."

The old man stares for a few moments, as if he had suddenly been struck by paralysis. But then he smiles patiently.

"No, you're mistaken. We met in the home of some nice

people, your parents. I took the liberty then of telling you about the Sabbath, our most important holiday, exclusively divine, when the Creator granted Himself a day of rest."

The old man hasn't lost the knack. I've got to give it to him, he is an educated man, in spite of the familiarity with which he stops passersby. But if he hopes for dialogue, he is fooling himself.

"I hoped you would understand that I am to blame if my daughter does not do homework on Saturday. I put it into her head. Learning becomes faith after a while—what could she do? I wonder, my son, if you've participated in the decision to expel her because of that. You would have had to. You had an important political role in your school. You were a group leader. They counted you among the believers, the soldiers, the killers. They gave you great power, dangerous power. Yes, yes. They taught you to enjoy this poison."

Really, he is fooling himself if he hopes for dialogue. No, he could not be stopped at all. Look, he is back at it again. "Yes, my pupil, were you silent when they took the decision? Perhaps you even spoke in favor of it? Unanimity, I know that all your resolutions are unanimous. Is it possible that you didn't catch her name, that you'd forgotten mine? Wischnitzer, that's my daughter's name, too! You aren't capable of such ugliness, am I right? Maybe you didn't even know her, my good boy. She's only thirteen, a mere child. Among our people, only the boys are men at this age!"

From the repair shop under whose eaves they had stopped, the loud sounds of a lathe invaded the street.

"Your parents asked me to instruct you. I refused for as long as I could. They knew about my daughter, what you had done. But they insisted. I couldn't forget your grandfather. No, I couldn't refuse him, my boy. Should I have brought this up at the very start?"

If this hoarse gentleman expects dialogue, he is wrong.

"You mustn't think that I'm judging you. I don't have that right. But I thought I'd take my leave of all of you, we're emigrating . . ."

The young man could bear no more. He suddenly awakened from his shock, hurt and angry, but the old man had disappeared.

"Didn't you teach me, comrade, that our daily history is a history of class struggle, that we have to fight the enemy at every moment, without illusions, without philistine sentimentalism? Without religious fervor, without childish feelings? No, I really didn't know your daughter, Comrade Berdichev. It is possible that I was there when the decision was taken. The little monster followed his mission, my dear instructor. He kicked out many. Didn't you teach me that judgment must remain above influence, unswayed? It must. One came from a bourgeois family, another refused to write on Saturday, and yet another joked about our saints. Yes, you are right, I tasted power. Yes, I swallowed the poison, my instructors hoped that I deserved this honor, this horror. . . ."

The stranger had left without offering his hand. Better alone! Without parents, instructors.

Grandparents, cousins, neighbors, aunts, instructors, parents; one after another, they leave the country. He smiled guiltily. Orphaned. He was alone on the street.

An extraordinary odyssey, yes, one that demands an inkwell. So he thought, the conceited little prig.

The cloud had descended over him; he was lost in it. But with that hellish buzzing in his ears, he couldn't concentrate at all on important thoughts.

He started off quickly toward the school, bent over, burrowing like a lathe through the morning fog. Now he began to run feverishly, besieged. His narrow shadow had come closer; it was filling the screen.

SUMMER

Every summer the city on the hill drowns in green, an explosion of green: on the grounds of the church, on the fortress, and
in the forest; while the river's green willows surround the city.

The summer of oaks and willows fans great invisible wings,
flapping on a surge of clear, pure air, torrid blasts of pulsating
blood; the cleansed, listless body is sucked from the ground,
lifted up and spun by astral whirlwinds. One can hear the quick
and powerful pounding of the chest; the eardrums thin out, the
arms hang and then come to life, the dewy eyes beg, the knees
are cold stone, the temples and head ache. But the body
breathes, greedy, relieved. The shoulders, the voice, and the
eyes are set free, the scorched, arid throat, the tongue licking
dry lips; the endless wandering, the long, hopeless wait for
somebody who will bring on summer's fugue; finally it comes
to others and to you, with the clear and high trumpet sound
raised at sunrise on the hill of the fortress. Every summer, and
yet differently this summer, the fever chooses another fool
for its ravenous and ferocious fury, for the fantastic smoking-
phosphorescence of the nights, the coldness of the insomnias.
This is a different summer.

For a whole week two years earlier the boy's timid smile had
overwhelmed the cinema screen; he alone had dominated the
white rectangle, with his red kerchief and his Pioneer uniform.

Rumors of this glory had covered the streets and the faces bathing in the golden green of summer. Once again the celebrations, the recitations, the speeches, the poems, the halo of a charming and precarious provincial celebrity. Then all that seemed to be over and done with: the well-pressed red kerchief was put away in a drawer with the towels and the handkerchiefs.

The rest of the summer was opaque; still, the little clown noticed that his glory was intact: he was seen with the same admiration and the same curiosity, he could go on displaying the same cinematographic smile everyone expected of him. So much for last summer; it dragged, it could have been said, through the sun-scorched dust.

And then the end. No, not quite. During the winter holidays he went—or rather, he was taken—to his first surprise party with grown-ups. He was welcomed like a star. . . . Barely minutes after they had taken his coat, the orchestra began playing a slow dance. It was up to the girls to choose their partners. Ten or so big girls, smiling and confident, crowded around him: Lia, Rodica, Mia, Ruth, Geta, a sulking brunette, and a certain Lucia who laughed all the time. He became confused; their hair was one undistinguishable mass. The star was flustered.

Then I felt Julia trembling near me; that's how the craziness began, all that madness, that is how I stayed with this group of boys and girls, two years older than I, in their senior year.

In the city they had forgotten neither the smile on the movie screen nor the peace poems he had served up during country festivals. The people no longer pointed to the hero, but they still continued to recognize him.

There were rumors that an excursion to the monastery had lasted until dawn, and certain young ladies were given a zero in conduct that cost them their prizes at the end of the year.

Tangled adventures covered up by the new summer, by the savage greenery in the forest or at the fortress, by the furtive trembling of the willows in the mornings by the river, where the summer's breathless whistle swelled up, where the water reflected the glances of swimmers until now chained to the dry shores of other seasons, stooped beneath their clothes, suffocated by the vigilance of neighbors and teachers.

In reality the landscapes receded quickly; the fortress and the river were of no importance, but for their feverishness, which tortured me at night, when the forest and the fortress and the river became mysterious, more alive, more dangerous than during the day.

The parents were content with their son's prizes at the end of the school year; reflected in their large bedroom mirror, their offspring looked like a mascot, a Chinese marionette, secretive, fragile, stubborn, comical, overwhelmed with medals, his hair parted neatly in the middle. In the eyes of the teachers as well, his hair was subdued, flattened, parted to the right and to the left, all the way down to the back of his shaved, pink neck, *but if I glanced once into the clear water of the river, or at Julia, into her limpid and clear eyes, suddenly my hair would appear wild, immense, curly—ever larger ringlets turning into untamable waves—"like Medusa's," as she had said. I looked at my chewed fingernails, I sucked their blood, I inhaled its smell and that of the skin of our young bodies, paralyzed by the silence and the crackling of the tormented bushes whose branches rustle with long, hushed whispers, as if trying to revive a quivering little flame.*

As evening fell they walked through the park. Not one bench was free. The whole group headed for the forest, each with his pussycat. Traian with Lia, Victor with Mia, Andrei with Radu and Titus, in the deaf brouhaha of playful caresses, Pupu with . . . yes, always with Rodica, and taking up the rear, Valeriu, mustachioed and sleepy. At a suitable distance from the group, junior strolled with the lithe, sensitive one, diaphanous because of her delicate lungs. The folly of their endless conversations with their rolled *r*'s. He avoided looking at her, but was bold enough to cover her shoulders with his new buckskin jacket.

The low, shaftlike, cavernous cinema had unsettled during the two hours of turmoil, of our hands groping at clothes, skin . . . if it had only happened there and then, in the dark swelter fed by hot breaths, when the bald man seated to our right was too absorbed in the B movie on the screen to be scandalized by what we were doing but didn't have the courage to do. "Let's go, I can't stand it anymore." Sure, but nearly two hours, entranced, as if exhausted by a séance from which we could have escaped only by jumping out of the window.

In the crowd that streamed from the theater, satisfied with its weekly dose of entertainment, the pubescent lover risked a gesture of tenderness: he took off his jacket to place it on the fawn's shoulders.

They walked in silence, apart. That is how they left the cinema and that is how the group found them: silent and apart. They had looked for a bench on the church grounds, but none were free. So, pensive and deflated, in fact somehow shrunken, they followed the others in the direction of the forest.

Evening. People recovered the vitality of the previous summers, they started to breathe the sky above, toward which they sometimes felt themselves rise to caress the contours of the moon.

The suitor was counting on the jacket he had laid over her soft, frail shoulders. He lacked both patience and nerve, the necessary brutality.

He refused to look at the sky: the moon yawned sarcastically. He forgot to breathe, plunged as he was into a hostile abyss, scorching and strange. He inhaled into his nostrils, into the emptiness of his chest, the vigorous air of the forest, a scent of firs that had given him vertigo two months earlier, when he had dared and she had let him . . . a kiss . . . Julia's hand had glided over him: thunderbolt at the speed of light, a jump without parachute, poignant scream of victory and intoxication, a scream he could not, of course, let out.

The folly of the letters had been going on for months. They had been discovered and read, of course, with shocked murmurs; he had seen the dumbfounded adults, the flush in his mother's cheeks. They didn't know that such compositions in fact delay the danger: the tender, photogenic archangel had fallen—foreseeably, therefore naturally—into the thin and fragile arms of a fine, cultured, tubercular girl whose vibrancy had devolved into adjectives.

Paralyzed for almost two hours in the darkness, in the midst of the whispers of the others, they did not move, made no attempt to touch. The girl seemed to prefer these delays. Or perhaps she didn't know what she was delaying, because this sensitive girl was also sensible. Or she knew only too well and took her time in order to savor the excitement for as long as possible, like a connoisseur, a seasoned expert. They got up right after the others left and walked to Julia's house without speaking. They remained mute and stiff under her window. Awkwardly he took the jacket from her shoulders. She didn't shudder; it wasn't until afterward, as the jacket slipped into his hand, that she brushed the leather sleeve and caressed it with her skinny, yellow fingers. It was dark; otherwise the rare passerby might have been shocked to see that the well-known face of the little orator and actor no longer resembled him. He walked slowly, with difficulty. At his house the lights were off. The key was not in its usual place on the windowsill, which could mean either that they expected to be woken up or that Lina was awake and would let him in.

But in front, in the kitchen, there was no light either. Surely a brief knock would suffice to wake her. She would open the door slowly, quietly, and everything would turn out all right.

He heard something or someone move; a rustle, or whispers, some more muffled than others.

Lina slept in the kitchen, in the so-called kitchen. From there he had to pass through the hallway and two doors to make it to his room.

She did not turn on the light. She opened the door cautiously and pressed up against her bed to let the boy pass.

Through the half-open door, the streetlamp shines on her blue eyes, her loose, damp hair, her low-cut gown that reveals a shoulder, the sweaty breasts.

She quickly closed the door behind him. Her hand was on the knob; she took a half step toward the door without moving from the edge of the bed.

For one more instant, a strip of light: the rumpled sheets, the khaki military helmet in the corner of the bed.

Total darkness, no movement. Only breathing and mingled odors rising heavily from the creaking bed.

The bed is to the right. I will brush against it; then the stove, then three more steps and then the door. Lina does not let me rest against the bed. She leads me herself. The sounds of breathing whirl through my head. Hers, mine, I don't know how many, I try to count them, they overlap, one, two, difficult to separate, another one, three, maybe three . . . Her hand is burning, slightly sticky; sliding, my fingers reach her warmish elbow. An acrid smell of damp sheets. The heavy stifling silence that I lie in wait for every night all summer long, from my room, where I will eventually be. Here is the first door; the sink is to my right. Three more steps; I am above the cellar. The floorboards arch up, creak. I touch the water heater to my left. Behind me I hear Lina, moving stealthily, returning to the rustling bed; I can hear some sort of murmuring.

I've arrived. I push the doorknob down all the way; I mustn't let it go. I open it. I know the technique well: you can't release your grip or let the knob glide up until the door is shut again. There, that's it, I'm in my room. I've closed the door, my bed is nearby, underneath the rectangular glass picture frame that protects the photomontage of my legendary campaigns. Tree branches outside let their shadows dance on the photographs; the young Pioneer wears a mustache now.

Night after night, back home, reeling, drained and feverish, in the abyss of insomnia, I listened to the hot and dark noises of the kitchen. My clothes, as always, folded over a chair, my shirt hanging on the peg, stretchers in my shoes, the branches' shadows on the photographs of the glorious Pioneer, that is all I saw while listening, until dawn, to the silence of the house. Nightly, in the fortress and forest of the kitchen, the restlessness of summer whirled sharp and dark, calling me, threatening me with failure if I continued to linger in the web of adjectives that stretched out the afternoons and tangled the evenings.

I don't need my pajamas, only my undershirt. Next door the parents sleep. Within their frames the photos move, the mustaches seesaw back and forth. The bed creaks. The silence weighs on my chest, my shoulders. I feel as if I were under a tank. I hear my breaths. For the two years that she has been with us, Lina has slept in the kitchen, on a wooden bed, right next to the door that lets in the cold during the winter.

Her bed creaks, I know it, it creaks loudly. The rumpled sheets smelled of sweat, but not only that: a sharp and sweet odor, of heat, but not only that: a burning dampness, something else, something sluggish, languid, a kind of sleepy smell, animal-like.

My eyes have adjusted, the darkness no longer wearies them. I listen to my breathing. It gallops, it whips the time that escapes me, and I cannot catch up.

Julia's skin, playful waters, refreshing, lips chapped, bitten to a burn. Each night the same madness, advanced a little, restrained a little; like a kettle under pressure, we empty ourselves of vapor. Lina's breasts revealed themselves, steaming, under the loose gown that slipped from her shoulder, and she swayed, languid, pushing me impatiently to my room.

The dead house, an endless wait, then I hear the key turn in the lock.

The door opens, where Lina is. Someone is coming in, no, leaving, of course. She is alone now, guilty, she knows it, she waits, she will pay.

I look for a cool spot in the sheets. It's warm, spongy all over. The pillow feels as though it were filled with lukewarm water. The room sweats disgust. The disgust of a false summer, of false past summers all revisited here today—a curse. The room is stifling, it needs to be tapped like a barrel, the indigo barrel of the night that must be shaken, be brought down, as the waiting must be shaken and dirtied, its mouth thirsting for saliva and blood, for heat, this mouth full of spuming adjectives. For a brief moment I still hear the falsetto murmur of simulated innocence, the breath burning with the feebleness of a consumptive. I will learn the movements, I will slip into the viscous, hot throat of the wild beast, gums vibrating, torrid, bleeding, greedy, watching for the fall of its prey. Finally lost, sold. That is to say, alive, devourable.

Silence. No movement. The knob must first be pressed down, then the door must be pushed. The steps beat in my chest, in my head.

I am above the cellar; the floorboards creak. To the right the heater, to the left the sink. My hand wraps around the second knob, presses it down.

Darkness reigns in the cage. I am next to the stove, one step. No one has moved. A muffled breath, but perceptible. I've been heard, perhaps awaited, a compromise: small price for my silence.

Blind, all I need is to possess the crater—poison of summer nights—in a lava of larvae and polyps. I sink in the cinema's white sheet, its illusory screen; it is swaying now, with me, damp and soiled, smelling and oozing, like me. Here are my feverish hands, the curls, the uncovered wetness, open to all promises, summer green darkened in the curled hair, phosphorescent with bacteria. I bite into the heart of her shoulder. Lina groans gently; finally I find Julia's lacerated lips, her skin of dancing waters.

The bitch's hot and hungry mouth raged, inhaled me, gulped me into its depths; the whirlwind heated my blood, invaded, inflamed by the soft viruses of summer. A tingling infected me with shame and savagery, with oblivion and disgust, and with pleasure, perdition, always closer, too close . . . in me.

THE TURNING
POINT

FROM THE window of the waiting room you could see the park. I was alone: in a few moments the door would open. It was almost noon, in the spring.

When I saw it for the first time it was about this same hour, many years ago, in the fall, about noon on a wet, windy day. It was lifting its despair to the sky. It roared, unabated, wounded, its waves rising to the mute and dark heavens, its bitterness pounding rhythmically against the unresponsive canopy.

A few months earlier I had entered the university. I had left my town, my home, my friends, my family. After the beginning of classes, the entire student body was sent off to do "voluntary" labor at a construction site. We slept in barracks, on bunk beds. We'd been outfitted with boots and jackets: we dug, pushed wheelbarrows, stacked bricks in mud so dense we had trouble pulling our feet out.

One Sunday they allowed us an excursion by train. It was a cold, breezy day. When we got off at the station the wind blew even harder, wetter, coming at us from all directions in the picturesque seaside town we were seeing for the first time. In the damp cold we walked along the streets of the center. The town limits didn't seem far away. In fact, after descending a number of winding lanes, we came to a stop.

That was when I saw the sea. It displayed before me its magnificent rebellion, its immense crash. I felt that I had been given something that could not be taken away, no matter how poor or dejected I might be. I was eighteen. I don't think I'll ever recapture that vibrancy again. I became speechless at the very moment I wanted to jump and shout and give free rein to extravagant gestures and words; I was dizzy with an extraordinary feeling that could not find release. This was something unknown but long awaited. I gave myself to it and found it frightening.

Subsequently, at unpredictable moments of the day or night, often even in my sleep, I felt an invigorating acceleration of my pulse, a sharpening of my senses. Something that had existed obscurely was awakening and opening up the horizon.

I COULD have returned to the seaside during the following weeks, but I never did. Not all returns could be as spectacular.

I came back, however. I had finished with my studies. It was summer, I had been married for two years. We were on a two-week vacation. My young sister-in-law, in her last year of high school, had come with us.

Once again I was breathless. I recognized the tension and gave myself up to it without inhibition. I jumped out of my skin. One simple syllable from my partner was enough to burst the surface electrified by the proximity to my source of joy and disquiet.

My companion was still suffering from the shock of her mother's suicide a few months earlier. She had neither loved nor understood her. She was still afraid of the surprises that, in her lifetime, the Party woman had sprung, from her high official post, on the family and strangers she controlled. The skinny, passionate student, pushed into marriage by her mother, who had an unexpected confidence in me, soon aligned herself with—or, rather, frantically clung to—her husband. A delicate creature, a brunette weasel with a taut, watchful, needy face. In a flash her eyes would light up and then just as suddenly darken, grow misty, a bulb of tears. An exotic madonna, torrid and frail, whose appearance could petrify a burning jungle. A feline, negative, twisted energy governed by the tides.

A young trio at the top of a cliff: evening, breeze, calm. The elegant young wife is suddenly stung by a poisonous breeze. "Why do you keep following us around?" she hisses to the shy one on her left. The nearsighted sister stops in her tracks, perplexed. She doesn't know how to respond. She could not have imagined such cruelty. She had been invited on this vacation, to help her get over the tragedy. It wasn't she who insisted that they go out together every evening.

Now the husband stops, his face in shock; he studies the two strangers between whom he has found himself, then turns his back on them. And, of course, his partner runs after her high-strung man. These were theatricals of a certain genre, informative about the stranger I then was.

The lava kept rising toward the mouth of the day's flames. We ran, heartsick, dazed, hypnotized, we struck out with our wings, teeth, and claws, and parted forever only to find each other again, a few hours later, in the same terror.

The young woman dissolved in the burning air of the shore. The languid blue sky instantly effaced every trace of her.

Then I saw her again sitting on a bench in the park: she was nibbling on sunflower seeds, a disheveled gypsy, a trafficker in tears and spicy pleasures. She waited, knees up to her chin, a greedy witch, flicking her long pink gazelle's tongue over her bare fragrant legs.

In the night her breasts swelled; she turned into a radiant Indian princess whose entrance silenced bands in nightclubs. Her metallic heels made dance halls palpitate to their rhythm. Her laughter erupted in staccato cascades, her teeth castanets. And at dawn, doctor, she became Scheherazade, and with the voice of a devilish Siamese cat spun strange tales, from life, naturally. I could have feasted on these luscious morsels of what you call happiness, but a narrow joy was all I discovered. I could sense that what awaited was a rigorously planned purgatory, postponed dreams, our equal slices of the rationed, productive future. I would have needed the strength to wish for more than was possible.

If one were to tell you about the sea, and about one's obsessions with it, the words would only too soon sound suspect. I feel accused. The obscure motivations, the uncertainty of even the most detailed evocations, cannot improve our dialogue.

I lose the energy to cross the barrier of speech.

Some time passed; hesitation nailed me to my seat, the silent room lost its therapeutic quality. Now what I see is a ponderous office of auditions and admonitions. This indicates that I have not come here of my own free will; the interrogation has been forced upon me; I answer to what I do not want to.

Yes, Mr. Interrogator, those were indeed different years. I was already a grown man. It was not a time of nebulous dreams, birds, waves, and black flights. In time a rapport with reality was established by, let us say, the need to regulate breathing. But of course this, too, could be called pathological. A previous consultation with one of your colleagues didn't go anywhere: "mental disorder," "fantasies," "evasions," the gamut of acceptable terms became a barrage of red arrows on the tongue of that severe pedagogue. What to do with a perfectly normal individual who has formed a natural, constant, and multileveled relationship, not with another person or an automobile or an Irish setter, but with a tree, or, why not, with the sea? Yes, that's it! And he listens as though to a madman. You happen to use a few terms, a few theories borrowed from *your* elusive discipline—to dare to decipher, even just a little, the bizarre state in which you aren't your everyday self but in which you are in fact becoming yourself, even if a little unreal. You are careful to avoid hypotheses and analysis, you content yourself simply with telling the story of the happy interludes; you tell it like it was, in order to explain that if this beneficial restlessness is an illness, it is also your only wealth, and they pat you on the back, recommend sleep, walks, or they stun you with pills.

There is nothing unusual, as you have said, in my viewing this mental confusion as a liberation. I admit it, I have used the word "freedom" too much. The sea awakened, it is true, an extraordinary need for it. Desire without an object, infantile longing, soon repaid by a feeling of freedom, somewhat idiotic, certainly, because I knew it couldn't last.

It is true, there were many nights in which I took part in exalted conversations. A few sensitive and responsible people had formed a secret and restricted group dedicated to an abstract restoration of dignity—abstract indeed, since our only aim was to learn to *think* again. We did not look for followers; we were isolated; we were skeptical, and there were only a few of us. We were looking for a bearable way of coming to terms with our own impotence, for humor and grace within the limits we'd already accepted and accustomed ourselves to—as is appropriate to mature men of sound judgment.

It has been said that the perniciousness of these nocturnal conversations during our holiday was proved by the infelicitous disappearance of one of our members. Witnesses were found who testified that she was of a mystical bent, because she was known to take the tragically irresolvable aspects of our arguments too seriously.

A truly mystical person would have had no need for our dialectical free-for-alls to persuade herself of what she is already convinced!

So when you say that you want to swim to the far shore, a distance of several kilometers, it may be a joke or madness or perhaps even an attempt to set a new record. Of course, suspicious zealots would view the *far shore* as a metaphor. Thus it is more appropriate to stick to the purely literal. My wife could have turned back halfway across, or she could, perhaps, have managed to reach her goal. No one can call them accidents before the fact: a storm, a heart attack, sharks, the undertow. You can't know what you haven't witnessed.

We were together, and we were on vacation. No one had better reason for knowing her than me. In spite of her irritability and frailty, she was an accomplished athlete, an excellent swimmer. It was not possible to predict what might exasperate or delight her. You must admit that even if it was an act of desperation, the cause must be sought in her character. Not necessarily in the heat of our debates, but in the boring details of everyday life. Any other interpretation would have to invent a link between this fatal accident and our nocturnal debates. At the meetings I may indeed have spouted some nonsense that we weren't allowed even to think.

These brief, illusory, heated exchanges were, why not admit it, all that was left of the infinite I had once hoped for.

If my humiliating confessions cannot put a stop to your interrogation, then I will have to send you to see a ghost. I know her address and I can show you the way. An autumn evening, cold, pouring with rain. It seems the end of the world, but only the initiates know it.

There is nothing to do but to take refuge in some small café or restaurant on the Calea Rahovei, a few steps up from the police precinct building, next to the pharmacy.

Ask for the manager: from her you'll find out more than from my stiff confession of principles! Look kindly upon the dignified matron. Talk, with this unlikely relative, about the suicide of the dark Party fighter who was her mother; about the tragic disappearance of her sister. You'll learn that it wasn't the sudden reversal of political fortunes that deprived her mother, that experienced fighter, of her maternal instincts.

She killed herself simply, quickly, with the same efficiency and dispatch of all her decisions. An urgent impulse, a random incision.

If, in the midst of her tale, she should be moved to tears, you stand a good chance of being regaled with tales of episodes predating her own arrival in this world. For example, what she knows about the dead child, the first fruit of a tempestuous liaison in her mother's youth: running late for a Party meeting, the highly strung woman had temporarily stored her dead baby in the refrigerator. An absolutely true story, very useful in the back-room strategy that brought about the fanatical woman's downfall. But it was not used against her just because it was true—it had, in spite of its clear-cut edge, a plurality of meanings, the irreducible ambiguity that characterizes each act in life, no matter how terrible.

The pitiful ball of grease (that is what the myopic girl of many years ago has turned into) will attest to my bizarre relationship with her mother, who chose me to play a part nothing had prepared me for. She knows how much I hated my mother-in-law, and also how she fascinated me. But the schoolgirl of twenty-five years ago forgot everything that has happened since. She doesn't understand why I detest, now more than ever, the weak employee I've become, the hostile sea that rejects us.

Take a good look at this soft gateau of a woman and you'll

understand what the shore signifies, now that there are no more promises. I hate her more than I hated her mother, because all that's left of her now is miasma and degradation and a clouded eye . . . and the sea that keeps retreating and no longer puts up with our failure and our humiliation.

I confess that the only transgression I haven't been able to rid myself of, in this steadily descending spiral of life, is my lack of faith in the charity of the authorities. I deny that anyone has the right to determine what is good or bad for me, and I no longer believe that my interrogator, never mind what he claims, has my "great possibilities" at heart, as you sustain.

Come to think of it, the accusations revolve only around a few words, rotten peels. I thought I could revive them, magnify, and shout them; I shed the tears of a megalomaniacal romantic over them. We were there, in the summer, naked, free, once again like children, stimulated by noble and impossible ideas. A truly democratic moment in which we became equal and silly.

A murmur, a hiss of childlike bravado, a vain stutter: it didn't go on for long! The rest of the time I functioned methodically and monotonously, quite proud of the fruits earned by labors that provided no relief and required no thought. My fellow salary-earners and five-year-plan followers saw me—rightly— as one of them. Things became worse when, several years later, words turned against me in an unexpected way, that is, they simply emptied themselves of all meaning. I ended up losing them entirely. They wouldn't have been of use, ill-suited as they were to the new era. Sometimes, however, I chatted aimlessly, with a kind of vehement indifference, do you remember? My former interrogator was intelligent, cunning; I was afraid of him because he was very experienced in this kind of thing. I haven't forgotten the stare of the bald and elegant beanpole whose dark and malicious eyes drilled into me, forcing me to look at his spotted forehead, at the impeccable lapels of his green suit.

After a few hours of interrogations with this veritable professor of behavioral science I found myself stooped, limited, determined to stifle all words and twaddle. I remember the words that I was called to account for, words that also brought me close to the cold and impassioned orator who later became, for a short time, my mother-in-law.

She seemed to know the mystery behind your faces rigorously molded by a hierarchical and precise technology. It was words, and their particular aura, that drew her and me together—and it was words, again, that drove us apart, irreparably. Even if you had forced me to bare my innermost soul little by little, I would never have spoken about the sea. But I was able to speak of it to her—and, what's more, it led to our brief and sad alliance! As if she had understood what I had confided to her, as if her rebellious pathology had only been the reverse of mine.

It was a complicity rather than a closeness. There always remained an area not covered, shifting—in the final analysis, an incompatibility. The daughter was eager to act on her mother's unspoken suggestion: she chose me precisely because she had perceived me as an ally.

Do words have a mysterious, unpredictable incandescence? Their magical inconsistency promises power, love, revolutions, inquisitions, and beliefs beyond our monotonous ordinary cycles. To turn and twist words can become a serious and remunerative occupation—like the one you practice.

It surely isn't an accident that words brought me to this little room of confessions and prayers. Here I can tell you how the summoning waves have continually changed colors and grown darker.

Pitifully, I have shown up at the torrid shore every year, with the same impotence and slightly sour nostalgia, unworthy of the vow I had believed myself able to keep the summer before. It was all right that the rest of the year was sheer deprivation, because my energies had to be mobilized and severely curbed in order to forget; otherwise, bang, there would be nothing left but a pile of bone dust.

I remember all the times the estimable Interrogator praised all that is alive. Like you, he had repeated firmly: there is nothing more important than life, only *it* is sacred. This is what a priest tells sinners.

And now the sinner attached to life has to convince his wise interrogator—priest, judge, pedagogue, pediatrician, whoever you may be—that the huge roar rising up to the stars, the nocturnal tumult of summers, finally represented nothing but death's gentle call.

THE HORIZON was no longer the same. It had become sarcastic, alien, aged.

Yes, that was despair, tall red whirlwinds rose out of the abyss, the mists whirled specters, avatars of death. I wandered in the regions of ancient lamentations, soulless and eyeless, estranged and old. All that had been exciting had proved perishable.

I have fought, however; honesty obliges me to make this lamentably vain statement. Hours of bread, and chains, struggling in silence, gritting teeth, refusing, harboring hatred, fleeing the noise of ovations that accompanied complicity and moral decline. It goes without saying that heroics were futile: the dragon's arms reached everywhere, they caught you and beat you down, time and again, until you finally learned the drumbeat of this place.

In the end, the inanimate, cold stone seems to win out by

absorbing us: we become part of the great moribund indifference, incapable of examining or opposing it.

I knew that in the coming summer something irrevocable
would happen. The web unraveled, knots came undone, mil-
dew spread everywhere. Even the fresh morning sky was
fraught with danger. At dusk, wild airborne creatures, their
eyes reddened by desire, exuded threatening liquids, arms of
flame. Teeth clenched, I spoke little. Sometimes I caught a
glimpse, in the eyeglasses of the lady who was now my companion, of my face tormented by premonitions. With a hiss of evil
augury the hour approached in which the beasts inside me had
to fight it out. The summer get-togethers of five years earlier,
of the year before, of the previous century, were no longer
possible. I glanced down at a magazine or at the lines of
hieroglyphs in books. I muttered a sarcastic refrain to the
always gracious and attentive woman—yes, gentlemen, one
might indeed say this, to the woman under whose protection
fate had placed me. I was busy distilling poisons, I admit. There
were tender silences, there was lyrical somnolence, there was
the soft pianissimo of evenings. Alone, I ran along the little
streets, sensing danger, hoping to have at least the relief of
howling before they came to get me. I would return nastier,
exhausted, tormented by the inability to slash and set fire.

The balance sheet was too hastily drawn, my explanations and
appeals too quickly refused. I certainly wasn't blameless. I didn't
have the strength to become a shit, the fight wasn't over yet, that's
what I wanted to say. But the due date had arrived. A metronome
had been set in motion. I kept on inventing excuses, shrugging
things off. I smiled at the sky and at my beloved, pretended to be
the master of the summer, master of the torments inflicted upon
me. I combed my hair regularly, brushed my teeth, but I could
already hear the trumpet, the gong, announcing the termination
of the contract, and the punishment to come.

*   *   *

END OF August—dead fish, coal, plastic boxes, bits of bird carcasses, pitch and rubber, shreds of paper, pieces of wood, jagged bits of metal washed ashore by a disgusting and furious sea.

For two weeks the couple sat on two blue towels, side by side, always in the same spot. The tourist community respects that choice and accepts the neophytes.

The others continue to observe them, but without insistence. The star stretches out sweetly, lazily basking in the summer's heat. The spectators guess she has, no doubt, forsaken the roars of the crowd in favor of this admirer—perhaps an archaeologist, or renowned surgeon or fashionable architect, who knows. She speaks with him in a subdued and discreet fashion; only the faintest, carefully coded expressions of intimacy reach the listener. The stargazers have to content themselves with the paradoxically protective role the distinguished Nana Mouskouri plays. Nevertheless, wagging tongues claim that the secret dynamics of every couple cannot be deciphered too quickly.

The sea kept bringing in offal, grease, pitchballs, foul-smelling wrack, fruit rinds, rags, empty cans.

Around eleven, the climbing of the hill to admire the view. It is rumored that a swimmer was pulled by the undertow and never managed to get back ashore. A young expert on catastrophes expounds about the dangers of a whirlpool only some hundred meters from the beach that can suck you into the depths and spit you out again far out to sea, whence there is no hope of return.

This could be a good opportunity for the couple to join in and take part in the hubbub. They keep too much to themselves. It doesn't do to be standoffish, or to amuse yourself by assigning malicious nicknames to the vulture with salt-and-pepper hair who you found out is a famous physician, or to his nubile chatterbox turtledove, or to the adulterous and photogenic viper who gracefully wags her thick hips past the bearded and toupéed actor, who is listening to the melodious confessions of a motherly brunette, a serious Italianate princess. It's a motley bunch; actress-mothers, celibate grandmothers, physicians, athletes, music lovers, bearded atheists and aristocratic flits, polyglot autodidacts and bohemian savants, all working at being casual on vacation.

The man often seems absentminded and remote. When his wavy black head of hair rises from the page of weeklies and dailies in which he has been engrossed, his expression could make you believe that he has just torn himself away from some weighty memories. The void in which he immerses himself— only to return from it distracted and inattentive—is of the kind that evokes mild feelings of irritation.

But, with a smile, the woman addresses kind words to the surly figure. He brightens momentarily, in little bursts of rebellious vitality, then folds back into himself, irritated, venomous, in the unfulfilled tension of last night and of the night before, their nocturnal emptiness. Under the sun by the sea his pulse is hostile, frenetic. The woman remains calm, comforting, and dispenses gentle words of advice. She is clearly content in her melancholic submission to laziness. A harmonious couple, one might say, joined in the inertia of recreation.

Saturday, end of August. The panic concerning the disappearance has proved to be unfounded. The hero has returned ashore and is immediately interviewed by his friends and people in the crowd. He has been coming to this beach for twenty years, he is a strong swimmer, knows how to conserve his energies, he is not afraid of the sea. If necessary, he lets the waves carry him, helps them along by gently paddling with his feet.

The tide keeps coming in. Waves roll onto the narrow pebble beach and lick the blue towel of the archaeologist, physician, engineer, architect, whatever he may be. In a swift, youthful motion, his distinguished lady gathers her hair at the back of her neck, the way she does on television, between songs. She puts her large sunglasses back on, adjusts them with her index finger in typical Nana Mouskouri fashion. Then touches, with a thin and gentle hand, the shoulder of her partner.

They have an instant understanding; the lean partner is on his feet in a flash. Nana readjusts her glasses with her right hand, just as in those artful pauses on the screen. She bends down, picks up the towels by their corners, shakes them, collects their big basket, his khaki bag, their napkins. They retreat one, two, eight steps back and to the side, and choose another spot. Nana rolls up her wet towel and they both sit down on his, which has remained dry, with the same pile of stuff beside them: a large willow basket, a khaki bag, the lady's red sandals, the gentleman's white thongs, magazines, napkins, tubes, a large black straw hat, a blue shawl, their white robes.

The inflatable cushion remains on the shared towel, under the goddess's delicate neck. Her companion leans on an elbow, perusing a book.

Saturday, end of August, an hour after noon. Blazing heat above a stinking, raging sea.

"I'd like to go in one more time."

"It's late, it's really time for lunch."

The distracted fellow hesitates for a few moments. It's quarter to two. Close to the shore, two high school girls disport themselves in the waves. The taller one is flawless and naked, perfect, like all banality.

The man looks at them, goes closer, walks into the water at an acceptable distance from them. The girls are now engaged in a mock fight. Back on the beach, Nana starts folding the towels. They had agreed on lunch at two o'clock.

He lets the swells rock him under the pitiless sun that hangs motionless in the sky. His head is enveloped in a crown of fire; long, dirty tongues of water lick his arms and body. The waves now reach up to his shoulders and neck, hold him in an embrace both oily and refreshing.

The surf tests its beat, and the foam rises, then breaks with the sound of a huge hand slapping down, a bomb fragmenting into wet, silky strands. His breath reaches out to the horizon: the body stretches, dilates, grows thinner, the delirious moment passes, the rush is over. While his head is aflame, soothing wet bandages envelop his arms, and he lets himself be held by them, saved, resting on the heights of the balancing, swollen, foamy wave.

The wave strikes, passes, withdraws. It gathers itself up, approaches, whines and roars, then disintegrates in a whirl that flattens out on the beach, withdraws, swells, roars, collapses in foam. A damp breeze cools his temples and shoulders; the sea goes slack and smooth.

He takes a step forward, forehead and neck in the sun, his arms in and part of the water. The joy of letting go! Another step, his foot rises, the bottom disappears. He turns, tries to regain his footing. It's just one step, he needs to take just one step back. He stretches his arms toward the beach. Then the sky is obscured by a wave rearing up like a huge ram above him and whirling thunderously down. Vertiginous, he is spun around at incredible speed. The blow is blinding, his hands flutter in supplication, but the wave now jerks him and tugs him out toward the great unknown. His feet fly backward, try to reach solid ground, but it has disappeared, there is nothing there but a soft, endlessly deep carpet. Above him a storm rages. He struggles, resists, exerts his hands and feet. He looks back at the shore, locks his gaze on it, resists the powerful pull into the depths, out to sea. Above him, foaming and rolling water—below his feet, the abyss. He spins around, terrified, tries to resist, falls, struggles. The current lifts him, turns him, tosses him into the mouth of the wave, farther out, over the crest of foam, ever farther and farther out.

He extends and contracts arms and feet, gets on top of the water, sinks again. He raises first one arm, then the other, reemerges: through the spray he can see the woman on the beach and the people milling around her.

Crazed, out of breath, he curls up, sinks, floats up, here comes the ram, a torrent of inky tar, he can't make it, no he can't, the water is above him, enormous, above . . .

But he tries, again, forward and up into the air with his arms, his head. Across the surface he can see the beach, he can see it all, but it keeps receding: the running woman, the shouts, the woman, the shouts, the beach. It's over, tonight she'll be alone, alive, alone, it's over. A spasm, ah, ah-ah-ah, he wants her, but that's just it, he can't have her, he raises his head out of the soft pillows but they fall back and over his face, they suffocate him, that's it, it's all over. What a stupid thing, why, why the hell is he here, submerged in water, pushed down into the depths, he can't get his head out, he gasps, he rages, he's getting too weak, he pushes with his head, arms, legs, hoists himself upward, and sees, it seems, sees—there they are, all agitated, he's seen them, they've seen him for sure, they're running, they're there, but so far, even farther—oh, so far, and now the sky is falling, the inky sky, he's a goner, it's over. . . . He gasps again, keeps on fighting, his hands his feet his eyes his neck his mouth his shoulders crushed, engulfed. It takes so long it takes seven, eight, eight, eight hours, or seven. Seven seconds, longer, much longer, a century—ah, but still, but still.

Fire, oh, water, desert tomb, water, alone, terror, the void, arm, leg, arm again, the high shore, so high—

Ah, to the bottom but still alive, ah ooh ah, oil, mouth, ears, throat, nails, oil, a push, in the air, who, it seems, someone, ah the wave, a push, a savior, ah, the doctor, the amorous vulture, one more arm, just one more, the wave, again the wave, nails, nails, at last closer, doc, my hand, here it is, take it, my hand, there, take it, don't let go, now don't grab too hard, just gently, just the hand! "Don't grab me, just give me your hand, that's all, just your hand!" I am dying, breath, bruise, hang on, hang on to the hand, hang on. He squeezes, squeezes the bony claw, panting, water in mouth, nose, throat, engorged by water, disgorging water, sinking, lost. The tar rises to the sky, groans and subsides, dark and oily. Rage in the battered head, the shore, they're galloping along the shore, the woman in red, in a red dress, or blue, the horizon red or blue embroiders the red white blue dress, the shore, I call out, there are calls, here he is, and here are others, three of them, three! They are pulling and pushing an air mattress, three men and a mattress! Panting, hissing, they try to lift the dead man onto it, pushing and pulling. Struck by the wave, they slip, they stumble, get up again, turn around, lift the rubber mattress, slip, pant, struggle at odds with each other. The milk boils over, eyes mouth nostrils, the spill is spreading, shit, urine, milk, gasoline, the sky a bottomless inkwell. The mattress, a plaything, a rag, I'm fading. Gripped by the claws of the vulture, he doesn't let go, is no longer capable of doing so, a slippery rubber hand in the doctor's claws who loses him, grabs him again, pulls him along, the wave is milk, tar, ink, and pulls, and look, there are four of them, even five, what sturdy lads these sailors are, a mattress, another mattress, another even grander hearse, it's a procession through the needle's eye. One hand, the other, anchored, one more time, try one more time. The bearded one to his left is exhausted, he sees him reel, livid, the rubber mattress tilts, shakes, tips over. Back in the soup, swamped, in front, in back, the water is leaping, they won't be able to hang on, the baby is sliding off the mattress tilting from left to right, the pallbearers keep changing places, handholds, hold on, hold on hard, the sea the waves the noise up above. "Take it easy, we've got you now, we'll make it . . ." The doctor hangs on to the dead man's left hand, squeezes it, doesn't let go.

Now, close to shore, the end! Spent, the pallbearers are exhausted, the waves wash over the neck, chest, mouth, over and over, eyes full of pus and sleep. They'll give up, let go of the cradle, let the child be reclaimed by the waters. They'll save their own skins, why keep on struggling, there's nothing to be done, that's the way it must be. They pant, and take deep breaths, their joints crack in exertion and terror, knocked about by the waves, bruised, blinded, wiped out.

A few more leaps, one more attempt to escape from the clutches of the sea. The arena has been roaring but now the audience seems paralyzed by emotion; silently it watches the combatants.

A final wave, fear, then up onto solid ground, and the athletes are standing tall on the sand. They lower their marinated trophy off their wet and inflamed shoulders to the beach.

Water streams from the heroes' heads and arms. The limp and battered child retrieved from the sea lies in his inflatable nest. The supporters gather in a circle with murmurs of astonishment and satisfaction. The circle opens to make way for a phantom, Nana Mouskouri, who hangs like a limp lettuce leaf on the arms of a couple of charitable vestals. The spectators note her wavering steps and dry sobs, so like those of a debutante.

The baby saved from drowning has no strength left for words. He raises one hand, the left, in a vague greeting, tries to smile. The athletes lift him up and carry him to his spot, where he flops, exhausted, onto the sand. They turn him over, head down, to rid him of the water, and as soon as his neck bends forward, it's as if a stiletto pierced his head in an explosion of pain.

They bring him a cup of coffee, an aspirin. And it takes just a moment for the curious to retreat to their previous positions, to watch from afar, to whisper among themselves.

It's the end of August, a Saturday, the time a quarter past three when the convalescent finally manages to respond to the tender care of the woman.

He has really died and been resurrected. A miracle. And the water returns, humming, caressing, drooling: frenetic waves, long lascivious tongues curling back into the depths, he's fighting them again, refusing to give in, attempting the impossible. His hand up in the air, to be seen and saved, in the midst of the hostile, gargling waters.

The narrow pebble beach lies below a high slope behind which the sun suddenly disappears at dusk. Slowly, taking long breaks, the couple climbs. They stop at every one of the steps carved into the clay and reinforced by stones. Little by little they ascend, slow down, stop. With each step they feel the sun getting closer up there above the cornfield. Below, at the foot of the slope, the beach lies dead under a grayish sky.

Tenderly the fragile woman helps her patient up the steps. At the top is the sun and the flaming field.

Taking frequent rests, they make their way on the dusty path winding its way around the cornfield, across the railroad tracks, to the village lanes. They enter the kitchen garden, and their hostess serves them their customary meal: soup, fried chicken, watermelon.

After a couple of forkfuls, the man saved from the sea retires to his room. The walls are decorated with dusty icons and old photographs, and on the bed is a colorful quilt. He closes his eyes, falls asleep. It is a deep, agitated sleep of almost two hours.

He stumbles, struck by the wave that returns, tall, venting its rage on his collapsed and defenseless shoulders. He shivers under the water-cannon striking his neck, his breath cut off by the breakers that attack him from all sides. Suddenly he raises his hands to his eyes, as if blinded by the chill of the moon in the window. You can hear the spasmodic drumbeat of the sea striking the shore. In the narrow window, the sickly moon looms closer.

Frightened and exhausted, they decide to leave the next morning. The express train pulls in, packed with passengers; there's standing room only. They spend the trip in the corridor, squeezed in among swarthy and talkative strangers.

The large rooms of their apartment, with their bay windows, feel like those of a sanatorium. They open doors and windows, take a bath, listen to a record. They fall asleep quickly, holding each other close—fearful but happy orphans.

Monday morning, and September is here. The town floats in soft autumn light. In the street a vacation feeling lingers—the firm stride of bronzed women, the southern cordiality of the men who have just returned to make small talk in their offices. Greetings, glances in the truce between seasons with its still-leafy trees and a harmonious and neutral sky above the lakes.

He ought to call the doctor, thank him. Nana has found out his name, and she also knows that he and his turtledove have returned. He really should call them, but he still doesn't feel strong enough, doesn't think he'd find the right words.

On Tuesday, around noon, he suddenly collapses in front of a coffee shop, struck out of the blue sky by something that seems to weigh a ton and causes sudden and pervasive pain. Riveted to the spot, he steadies himself against the window, then hails a taxi home. The driver helps him into the elevator, from the elevator into the apartment, from the door to his bed.

Later that afternoon Nana calls Dr. Chelba, the savior. The

vulture recognizes the soft and inimitable voice immediately; he says he'd be delighted, he'll be there in half an hour, no problem, don't mention it, it's his duty.

The fever lasts a week. The patient is unable to move; the slightest twist brings on pains in his chest, shoulder, abdomen. Neuralgias, stretched muscles, gastric infection: all are treated in turn. "It's unbelievable, isn't it, what has become of our beaches. It's disgusting! Last year I saw—please excuse me, madam—but I saw these *shit-floes* all along the beach. I could only swim once. And that awful Saturday there was a storm, too. Just imagine the broth you must've been swallowing!"

The patient's breath is shallow. Infinite precautions need to be taken when he wants to change his position or raise himself up. The pain does not subside, and the injured stomach refuses nourishment, as though it were swollen by worms.

It takes him weeks to get well. He sleeps fitfully, keeps waking up with a start, his hands on top of his head to ward off blows; groans and spasms, bed spins—his body crumples the way a drunk's does when he can no longer stand the circling of the walls.

"In fact, I've just barely escaped death. Only a reprieve, to be sure. Do I now feel capable of accomplishing more? Have I become more detached, more cruel? Whatever seems arbitrary may also turn out to be for the best, and I'm sure that's the case with me, too. Maybe I'll even find it easier to give up things, if necessary. When I stepped out to see you, I thought I noticed, on a dark street corner, an excessively well-dressed gentleman following me. Recently I've begun to find such occurrences common. If that tall, blond, elegant fellow should, for example, tell me that they've decided to expel me, I'd accept the decision without demanding an explanation. I would only ask to be sent, not to the paradise of happiness nor to the country of all freedoms nor to a holy land, but, let's say, to Dahomey. I'd get a job as a cashier at some zoological or botanical garden, among people with whom I couldn't exchange two words. Tolerated, remote, vegetative—completely anonymous in the African furnace. I'd be ready to leave at a moment's notice and instantly forget all unfinished projects, memories, feelings. I'd be content with the sun, the beasts of the jungle, cheap women, my own sweat. But this may well be idle talk."

"Oh, but my dear man, you've been extremely resilient! A very rare case: not to know how to swim, yet to survive for such a long time! It's a sign of a great thirst for life. Such tenacity! You even managed not to swallow all that much water. And you kept such a clear head! I told you to give me your hand without grabbing too hard—that would have forced me to let go of you. Which is what happened to me three years ago, with a woman—she was swimming in the nude, got carried away by the undertow. I saw it, I jumped in. I couldn't grab her by her swimsuit, since she wasn't wearing one. She got a stranglehold on me, we started sinking. I had to disengage myself, get away, or else both of us would have drowned. And, you must realize, she was a friend! I saw her drown right in front of my eyes. But you, you remained lucid. You're not the elegiac type, you're clear-headed and strong."

On and on about lucidity and resilience and so forth! And the goodness of the water raging over me. Right over my head, roaring. Soon, maybe, the water up above again, redemptive. Once again raise an arm out of it . . . no longer with such despair, but simply to wave farewell.

Elegiac? Maybe. And yet it's not the weaklings but the clear-headed ones who understand, the resilient ones who have the strength to admit that there is no solution, none whatsoever! They can't resign themselves, they transform their refusal or outcry into a kind of call addressed to no one, like a prayer, like the delirium of sleepwalkers or of the sick, like the words that escape during sleep, delirium, love.

No one would have thought that he regarded himself as only partially returned to reality, faced with a longer punishment, over a low flame. But the physician was a pleasant person to talk to, an enlightened man who exuded a comforting sense of male camaraderie.

Little by little, the days and nights returned to normal. Everyday life compensated for the deficiencies, flattened out the kinks, slowed him down to the steady thin vibration that always seems like a straight line. It's only when the heart stops that the oscillations disappear from the screen, when the final point slides down to the horizontal, toward perfect stasis. Despite his recovery, his pulse still indicated some vaguely suspect fibrillations; adding these up, one got the asymptote that alone distinguishes those infinitesimal differences, which at first seem to be caused by an error of reading, from the calm horizontal.

So it wasn't extinction yet; it was possible to reconstruct the ascents and the descents, the mysterious voids, the expectation, the flash of the fatal dart, the red point of rupture on the curve, the inflection that suddenly changes the sense.

Soon enough the employee falls back into his old routine. His seemingly indifferent and apathetic eyes take in more than before. The days and nights bleached out by boredom and diminution are more visible on the faces of others—in their measured gestures, in their silly and furtive little jokes.

He spends his afternoons studying volumes of rules and regulations, instructions detailed down to the last: when to take your vacation, how to use electricity, what needs are covered by the average salary, how long to keep a jar of plum jam, why one must not drink, not smoke, not get excited, not, not—what are the duties of some and the benefits of others, and about property, and about mothers of numerous children, and the tax on infertility, and the quota for the parks. When he's had enough he leaves the library and goes out into the street to look at faces. He is particularly interested in those of drunks, housewives, drivers, beggars, children, deaf-mutes, crooks, agents, cooks, gypsies, schoolteachers. He watches for deviations, brief terrifying explosions when normality is detonated and becomes delinquency—this one has left his wife, that one has moved to another town, said good-bye to the factory, the organization, the theater, the barracks.

These signs force one to abstractions. But he postpones, preferring to contemplate, over and over again, the furrowed brows of those wounded by reality . . . the syndrome of uniformization and fakery; revery and thought elevated so high that they can no longer be reached. Frequent exercises in taking positions, another routine, pages and pages on his own impasses. Melancholic habits, the hygiene and despair of the perennial everyday, everything functioning so well in the void that one hardly has time to notice before everything has reassumed the lazy course of submission—that everything has, in other words, returned to normal.

Once again he accepts the lines at the dairy or bakery, finds himself jostling other buyers of newspapers. Once again he gets on buses bursting with damp bodies. Sometimes he visits a shop that has nothing but nails for sale. One rainy evening he notices he is once again carrying a shopping bag full of bottles: modest labels, fake "natural" names for rotgut he'd long ago promised himself never to touch again. As before he greets his boss, tells him the latest jokes about the great buffoon. He acts indifferent when someone looks at him too insistently or when he is severely reprimanded for having spoken his mind, and, just as before, he neglects to notice the minute changes in products, prices, jargon—the mute subtexts of everyday life, the gray fog into which more and more of them are vanishing. One thoughtless evening he turns on the television set and slumps into an armchair. One indifferent stare, and he's hooked. His only resistance is definitive exhaustion; he doesn't even have enough strength to turn the thing off. The abyss gapes in the weary and stupefied soul of the televiewer he has once again become. Horrified, he recognizes the old exhaustion that dissolves all thought and motion. A poor fool denied pride of spirit and action: that's what he had become once again, so quickly. Sad but irrefutable proof that he has been resurrected, that he was alive. Is this the shock of readjustment? Life gave him back his reflexes, his grimaces? He was back among them, and for good, he knew that. The frustration that causes sudden migraines, that stifles every cry and tear and makes it sound false, subdues all glorious folly—the familiar cycle, the barrier he'll run into again and again, sulking like a child.

The elevator in his building, of course, breaks down almost every day. On Wednesday he will see his overjolly colleagues again, the town squares teeming with schoolchildren in uniforms, the official carnivals. The well-groomed saleslady at the tobacconist has become more and more aggressive and no longer saves his favorite brand for him. The radiators are hissing, people are rushing around buying blankets and sweaters. The downtown churches and photography studios are packed; the suburbs invade the metropolis for their formal weddings, bulk baptisms, first communions, and funerals galore. In the evening the city switches its lights off early. Night sets up command posts and sends crooked and suspicious shadows flickering against the walls. Rejuvenated retirees come back from their trips with senile smiles. Auto mechanics acquire the prestige of academics; dance tunes from the collective farms and pompously nonsensical news reports fill the airwaves. The powers of the apartment complex manager increase, and the tenants flatter him. The price of videocassettes goes up, and people are growing Teutonic mustaches and long Viking hair. Female students reject the bra. It is a grand period for the monumental arts, operetta, and philately. More people take up chess and needlework. The administration encourages the production of canned turnips and rutabagas. Ancient hymns are back in favor, lullabies are declared pedagogically sound. War is waged against parasitism, hooliganism, and sophisticated tastes. Dialect has vanquished dialectics. Behind their masks, the pedestrians are chewing gum. Women's and men's Wellington boots are standardized, toilets on trains are abolished because of environmental concerns. Restaurants only take group bookings. It has been decided to promote choral singing, old proverbs, simple food; games like croquet and bridge are back in fashion; the cafés close at eight, and so do the cinemas.

Garbled words, crazy words, returned by newspaper readers to the gaping maw of the days whence they emerged, puffs of smoke and flecks of spittle, just right for recycling in small talk with one of your mother-in-law's friends, the lady of the house at her loom, or the neighbor with his ear glued to the wall, eager to detect listeners to forbidden broadcasts.

During the first days of humidity and cold, after having suddenly seen, one morning, an unchanged face in the mirror, one that looks as if nothing had happened, the employee finds time to persuade himself that his gestures have remained unchanged and that his words are the same as ever.

"What a fine evening—really marvelous!" he proclaims, entering a tea room in mid-December. "It's winter, I can't drown now! Never mind that I was cast back ashore. Why should I go on looking like you, with your eyes glued to the floor? I'll try it again, just wait. Flunkies and jails be damned. I'll do it quietly, carefully, make no sound." The last words in a whisper, strictly secret.

What to do, what to do, he stutters to himself, wedged

between sweaty bodies. It's back to normal, to such brutish stammerings, buffeted right and left on the morning bus, what can one do, what would one do if one could? He catches himself in order not to be found out; once again he is courteous and accommodating to his superiors, his wife, punctilious in his tasks, full of confidence, recovered—ready for these journeys, for the stale stench of the offices, the gossip, the bowing and scraping, the lines at the grocery store, the dry goods store, the bad jokes, the crises, all the things it takes to survive. In the evening, a tender moment of release. Still frail and dim of sight, he reaches out for her, the woman whose gentle voice is heard in the apartment a few times a week. Sometimes he even has the strength to study his wrinkles in Nana Mouskouri's glasses. The woman's lenses shrink the face of the bearded adolescent, freeze the staccato laughter of an old man.

In short, he accommodates himself to his generation, rejects the tragic, trivializes everything. The hours are accounted for conscientiously, the rare moments of idleness open up into a chaotic void in which he feels stupid and finds it difficult to make any move at all.

He returns to old fare, old books. The pills and the pajamas are the same; he recognizes the streets, his office, his friends' voices, the gestures of the woman who is his companion of late.

Nothing reminds him of the forgotten accident or his dim premonitions: besides, no one ever mentions it. The following summer, without consulting his partner, he changes the itinerary of their vacation. It will be in the mountains, a neutral place without a story, precisely what so many people find blissful (such, for so many, is happiness).

SUNSET. EVERYTHING blends together. He no longer remembers the morning when roaring whirlpools tossed him like a colorless leaf. Lying on the couch, eyes closed, he woke up again at the end of another day, hands raised as if to chase away the shadow that rumbled above his head. He protected himself like a child, trembling hands warding off the crooked black beak. It only lasted a few moments. He calmed down, wiped the sweat off his forehead and neck. It had just been the memory of the water, he could still hear it inside his eardrums—a soft, insistent hum he wasn't able to get rid of.

This had also happened once when he was walking up the stairs, once when he was studying the names on the communal bulletin board, and once when he heard, at close range, the deranged voice of a drunk shouting his grievances. And on another day, when he ran into a group of people milling around a fire hydrant by the streetcar tracks. At noon, at the office, bent over his papers, or in the morning, in the bathroom, where he suddenly froze, toothbrush in hand. There had even been times in his dreams when the wave had taken him by surprise. There had been no time to react. Contorted, stunned by the rushing sound of the faucet, he tried to steady himself by grabbing the counter, or the door handle, or the edge of the bed that was swaying and tumbling, a nutshell buffeted by the rage of the tempest.

Nevertheless, these attacks, which usually ended in vomiting and apathy, grew gradually less frequent.

One day he made the paradoxical decision to counterattack. He did it without hesitation, in a serene and determined mood. He called the physician who had saved him from drowning and without any polite preliminaries asked him about the hours of the swimming pool that the eminent doctor visited twice a week. There were swimming instructors there, the water was clean, not too many people used it—perfect!

He slipped quickly into his new role, that of a mature student, a bit ridiculous among boisterous teenagers and a few retirees who tended to be overly enthusiastic and talkative. He

managed to ignore them. He attended his lessons conscientiously and in a few weeks acquired the knack of breathing and
moving in a coordinated fashion. The instructor, a stern, pot-
bellied fellow with a mustache, expressed satisfaction with the
progress of his taciturn student, who felt that his goal had been
reached when he managed two lengths of the pool without
stopping. He was made to join the gentlemen who did their
weekly exercise in the adjoining gym; the old vulture was there,
too, and their conversation took a pleasing, amicable turn.
They met at concerts and at the record shop: the doctor was a
sophisticated music connoisseur. Little by little, the Calvary of
his stifling working life, the narrow and tortuous tunnel of
confused expectations with its endless discontents and schemes,
became contained in therapeutic parentheses. He discovered
that there was a way to ignore reality—a regimen of enjoyable
evasions, music, sports, friendly pieces of armor that allowed
one to be absent, to be distracted. This did, of course, require
discipline, a sense of humor, and a measure of egotism. He
wasn't quite sure if he'd have the strength to maintain for very
long this tonic way of estrangement; neither was he sure that
the explosion, after so many evasions and postponements,
might not result in an even more dangerous breakdown. Nevertheless he adapted himself satisfactorily to this "indeterminate
solution," as it was called by the doctor, who tried to convince
him that in this way he was not evading the essential but was
reinventing the possibility for an authentic and substantial life.

For a while the new armor helped him endure sacrificing his
working days to nothingness.

One summer day he decided to return to the vacation cottage and the distant beach. He felt he was ready and set out in
a hurry, without emotion. He got there in the afternoon. He
took lodgings with an old woman who had only one room to
rent: this suited him, as it eliminated any dealings with neigh-

bors. He spent the evening in the room and went out late, after the whole village had been plunged into darkness. One had to watch one's step on the dark streets with their numerous pot-holes and large rocks in the roadway. Slowly, like a blind man, he veered to the left, the direction from which the quiet, sleepy murmur of the sea was heard. He knew he'd chosen the right path when the sound of waves breaking on the shore grew more distinct, but decided to keep his distance from it and contented himself with listening to the sea's nocturne from afar. He felt perfectly calm. He returned to the room, whose white walls were decorated with icons and photographs, had no trouble falling asleep, and woke up in the morning refreshed and in a good mood.

As before, the narrow pebbly beach had attracted only a few small and disparate groups. He spread out his towel close to the water's edge. The sun was shining through a light mist, not too hot, and the sea was calm. His doctor friend must not have arrived yet. As before, the place had the feeling of a peaceful refuge. The naked bodies radiated a kind of camaraderie, an ingenuous complicity, a small defiance against restrictive customs: women and men rid of their garments; a discreet transgression; a modest seasonal liberation. It was a kind of therapy of neutrality, surprisingly free of stress.

For a few days he didn't go in the water but looked at the sea from time to time with an indulgent and innocent smile. He avoided even casual conversation with the other tourists. Alone, his newspapers and magazines spread out around him, he contented himself with contemplating the shore and the calmly awaiting sea.

Toward noon the sky clouded over. Suddenly, without hesitation, he took a few cautious steps into the water, which enveloped him gently and rose cold over his shoulders. Another step and he lost his footing. The water took him, covered him,

turned him around. He put up an exaggerated show of splash-
ing around and raised his head out of the water. No one on the
beach seemed to be paying any attention. He huffed and
puffed, grunted, spat out jets of water, slapped the waves. He
turned on his back and floated with only his nostrils above the
surface. He dived down, came up again. There seemed to be
some mild agitation on the beach. He dived again, all the way
to the bottom this time, and came up again slowly to float,
victorious and at peace, on the mirror-surface of the sea.

He repeated this parody on the following days. His audience
quickly got used to his childish games, even when he performed
them farther and farther out, on the open sea, adding new
refinements to his leaps and dives. In effect he could have
drowned; certainly he was not the accomplished swimmer he
pretended to be. It would have been impossible to prevent the
accident. The spectators would have thought it was another of
his games, which they were already observing with annoyance.

One evening he saw his body in the long, dirty mirror of his
room. It looked burned or flayed, like some bizarre parody. He
examined his hands: they were intact. But on his neck and
forehead there were these asymmetrical, elongated blotches of
white.

He didn't leave his room for the next two days, but the marks
remained. Perturbed, he packed his bags and took an evening
train. He arrived at his apartment late at night, slept soundly
and for a long time, and woke up around noon the following
day. He examined his skin: the marks seemed to be growing
fainter. This impression was confirmed in the afternoon—they
disappeared. The white areas slowly regained their coloration.
After a few more days it was hard to see any trace of them.

He called the doctor. Was it the dirty water, some bizarre
allergy? No, the water had been clear and clean. "Why not go
back?" asked the doctor. "If you'd like to come with us, we're

leaving in two days." Since he still had two weeks of vacation, he accepted the offer.

In the train compartment, the vulture, the turtledove, and their two offspring were pleasant and amusing company. The trip went by in a flash, and that afternoon he was back in his lodgings with the same old peasant woman, who hardly looked up from her gardening to welcome him but simply pointed at the door of his room, as if she'd been certain he would return, or as if she hadn't even noticed that he'd been gone.

The doctor and his family had arranged to come pick him up on their way to the beach the next morning. He stood by the door and watched them approach, walking two abreast, the little girl trailing behind the vulture, the boy a few steps behind his mother, carrying tent pegs, bags, balloons, kites, a whole colorful array of things.

The day started out well, the sun not too hot, the sea calm. He picked a spot close to the narrow end of the beach. The doctor's family proceeded to renew old acquaintances, holding court, ignoring him where he lay on his old blue towel, his head on a small yellow inflatable cushion. The sky was misty, peaceful.

"You're not going in?" he was asked in turn by the doctor, the turtledove, and their son—who was, he found out, an aspiring pianist.

"No, maybe later," he mumbled and returned to his siesta.

Toward noon the sea darkened, grew agitated with a distant, muted roiling and small gusts of breeze from off the horizon. The sun was still shining through a whitish spider's web of mist.

He didn't go into the water that day but walked back slowly to his lodgings, ahead of the others. The painstaking examination to which he submitted his body in the room that smelled of old things and lavender revealed some almost imperceptible discoloration of the skin on his arms and shoulders, as if someone had been flaying him but starting out small, with perfidious cunning.

He didn't go for a swim the next day, either. The weather remained pleasant. He spent longer hours lazing on the beach and returned with the others, at sunset.

Back in his room, the white spots looked larger. In the evening he went for a walk with the model family. They sat outside late, peasant-fashion, on a bench in front of the door, chatting about this and that.

He woke up at dawn and descended to the yard, feeling refreshed. The air was cool, the flowers fragrant in the garden. He fetched water and washed his whole body, which was now entirely covered with large white splotches. They'd also appeared on his neck, his chin, and his forehead. Depressed, he sat on the edge of his bed for a long time, absentmindedly stroking the peasant bedspread woven of rough wool. Then he stuffed his few belongings into a bag, left the money he owed on the table, and went home.

The following summer he came back for a week. The symptoms reappeared quickly. He gave up but returned in early autumn. The weather was good, the sun still had some heat. There were fewer people, since the vacation season was drawing to an end. The spots reappeared the next day. His right hand was gloved up to the elbow with a fine web of loops large and small. His neck bore the imprint of a hand, as if someone had tried to strangle him. His torso remained unblemished, but below the waistline the irregular-shaped splotches began again; his left knee looked as if it had been wrapped in gauze or sheeted in aluminum. A clown's plagued outfit hired for a season at a colorful and foul-smelling Oriental bazaar.

Undaunted, he once again indulged in his eccentric water games, dived noisily into the sea, sought the bottom, let himself be pummeled and enveloped by the surf. Drained and indifferent, he resurfaced, out in the open waters or close to shore, then paddled to the beach like an exhausted old woman. Several times a day he went back to his frenzied antics, always teetering between self-irony and serious risk, and once again was gripped by occasional rages that originated who knows where.

Soon he'd had enough of these pranks, and on his last day he just sat there and said farewell to the horizon from which he had become estranged.

Back home, he buried himself in his monotonous schedule, accepted the sullen and artificial way in which it shredded his days. Regular habits, normal pulse. Step by step he advanced from acceptance to commendation to promotion, and made himself more at home in the diligence of industry and reward.

His increasingly restrained and conventional behavior evoked no surprise at all among his friends or relatives. Among his colleagues, with whom he spent a large part of his days, the change went totally unnoticed. After a while, once he'd become so accustomed to this new self that he no longer felt any recurrence of the old perturbations, he started asking himself if he wasn't missing something: perhaps he should pay more attention to those close to him? Surely they must have shown—if even just for a short while—some natural curiosity? He realized that he hadn't in fact seen any of his old friends for a long time. Little by little he had also withdrawn from his few relatives who were still alive. Gently, he tried to get back in touch with them, but it didn't really work. He would see one or another of them, but only very occasionally.

After some taciturn and polite reunions that he was soon to avoid altogether, he dedicated himself to closer observation of his colleagues. In most of them he recognized changes, almost imperceptible, that were different from his and yet corresponded to them in some sad, obscure way, as if everyone had reacted, according to his or her temperament and opportunities, to some diffuse threat that was gradually becoming clearer and more persistent: just as, after an initial unnoticed stage, a kind of incubation period, air pollution begins to cause migraines, asthma, bronchial problems—or, rather, a kind of perennially fleeting lethargy, none too definite yet clearly hostile, aggressive, and too late to cure as soon as it has declared itself. At one time he'd been only dimly aware of the symptoms; often, potential maladies only manifested themselves in their incurable chronic phase. Perhaps this was the consequence of aging, but they couldn't have all grown old at once! There are many old people who resist the decline vigorously and show no sign of such humiliating indifference, but instead are energetic, optimistic, as if the race had only just begun.

Now he thought he understood the reticence of his old friends, the laconic and stilted dialogue with his relatives. He didn't mean much to them because nothing and no one meant much to anybody in the final analysis, that is also how he felt. He had drifted away from them, not because he'd lost interest in one or the other of them, but because he'd lost interest in himself. Many, if not all, had undergone such a confused retrenchment.

It's a shrinkage, doctor, a kind of slowed-down metabolism, down to a quarter of its potential. A resigned, senile attitude. A partial faint, an existence between sleep and waking. But I was working, was producing, was advancing, in a semihibernating state, up to the lunch break, the evening, the weekend, the payday, the vacation, the retirement, the silence, the peace everlasting! Poisoned or crushed by something invisible, enormous, with a miraculous power to discourage them even before they've tried anything, as if they couldn't find salvation except by squeezing themselves into a gelatinous shell, tight, vaguely tepid, where they couldn't expect anything but a dull postponement that seems—believe it or not—comfortable to them, in their diminished sense of their own worth. Well, there's the elegiac for you, doctor! We have lost our vital instincts, my dear sir, no doubt about it, we have become elegiac. The epoch has flattened us. . . . See here, doctor, I've created a graphic representation of all this, with its points and trajectories and all. I have noted ages and occupations of people I know in order to find an envelope for the curves, or as we say in geometry, a cumulative synthesis—not least in order to discover myself, as well. To see where the curve changes, how, when, and why, to understand myself through the others, and in relation to them. The turning point where the funeral march becomes an elegy—which is followed by the polka, the tango, the accordion of jolly requiems. The point at which my curve has changed direction again, made an upward turn.

You remember this little restaurant, my friend.

At the tiny little place that used to be a secondhand shop that used to be a tavern that used to be a pastry shop, the young girls on their stools stopped their chitchat as soon as the elegant customer entered. The plump comrade manager appeared, smoothing her shiny black hair.

"So you really don't recognize me?" asked the distinguished gentleman about half an hour later, after they had consumed a couple of drinks.

Neat beard, old-fashioned manners, good clothes—a gentleman, no doubt about it. The somewhat intimidated comrade restaurant manager fidgeted with her dress.

"Of course I remember you—recently, you've been here with the doctor," she twittered.

"That's right, this is where we stopped in, on our walks. He taught me how to go for relaxing strolls, the good doctor did, but he also asks a lot of questions. Too many questions, Tania. I have known you for a long time. After we knew each other, you began studying law. . . ."

The fat little woman opened her mouth in shock, showing her yellow teeth. She fumbled for her glasses in her purse.

"Yes, the juridical sciences, but I had a hard time with it, wasn't really cut out for it. Me, a judge! But I did come from a good social background, although my poor mother . . ."

"I know, I know, I understand," said the stranger, soothingly.

"I couldn't do it, I would have judged in my own way, the right way and the wrong way, and what's more, I let myself feel pity."

"Oh! I remember, you had these weaknesses even in your youth."

The gentleman refilled their glasses again.

"But now you're here. Do you like it here? Do you feel good about it?"

"What can I say? I've had my setbacks. Someone found this job for me. The girls are sweet, we're like a family. I can even say my prayers, no one bothers me about it here. And I've always loved working in the kitchen."

"I remember your puff pastry! And your vol-au-vents, your Genoese pastries, your tarts—Tania's famous cheesecake."

These last kind words had a devastating effect. The woman grew pale and started to rub her temples with her hands.

"Oh, my goodness! Oh, dear," she exclaimed, making the sign of the cross. "How could I have forgotten? Oh, my! Not to have recognized you!"

She raised the glass of cognac to her lips, her large near-sighted eyes brimming with tears.

"You know, it gives me the shivers. Seeing you brings back my poor sister—she's found peace, I hope—and that dead baby my poor harebrained mother allegedly put in the refrigerator. What an idiot, to bother you with that. But you have changed so, the beard, the suit . . . oh my, what was I thinking of!"

They had another drink, and another. The treacherous golden liquid released them from their inhibitions. They smiled at each other. Comrade Tania could hardly restrain herself from running over to the girls to tell them about this surprise, just imagine, girls, oh, my! She wiped her damp hands on her gleaming black chignon.

"And what have you been doing since we . . . how have you done in the world? Quite well, I can see. I'm glad."

"Yes, dear Tania, the invisible doesn't count, you're right about that. Let's stick to plain narrative, to the chapter headings in the personal file. Your formidable mother got away from us, all right, when she decided to get away from everything. Those were the early, confused years. They didn't hurt me more than they hurt others. I'm a thrifty person, I have a good tailor, I obey traffic rules, I work hard, I put on weight but don't show it. It's a generous, seductive country, and we could have lived a fun little life, like all those who laugh and don't expect too much. Where did it all go, what happened to all our . . . The field lies fallow, we can't regain the most natural thing of all, the breath of life. But tell me, do you still go to the seaside? You remember that day when . . ."

"That's better forgotten! Why would I want to go there, don't you see . . . But it's just as you say, the field lies fallow. . . ."

She repeated the words in a pious tone, impressed by the lofty language of her customer, who had almost emptied the bottle. Although it was chilly, he had unbuttoned his overcoat and was getting angry about God knows what. He started muttering.

"I was given a warning, wasn't I? I really almost drowned. Was told not to come back. And there's nothing there for me anymore. Yes, no two ways about it, the sea rejected me, drowned me, defiled me."

He was ranting at the void now, quite out of character for such a distinguished gentleman. He tried to light a cigarette but couldn't manage it. Tania just sat there like a saint, oh my oh my, she tapped her lips with her fingers to keep herself from saying anything inappropriate. When someone's in such a dark mood you mustn't . . .

Yes, doctor, this is the story, there's no hope left, yet one wants to give up, so one acts like a clown, performs somersaults and pratfalls. It's not for lack of trying, doctor, he had said one evening when he ran into the doctor—his friend and savior whom he hadn't seen for a long time—outside a restaurant on the Calea Rahovei.

A fine evening, cool and quiet. One could speak freely, as indeed they did, seated at a table outside a shabby restaurant on the outskirts of a new housing development.

Those phantasmagoric dreams, the misty yearning for far-away places, the colorful, treacherous twists and turns of abstract speculation—it goes without saying that I never found my way back to those.

Duplicity and masquerade, that's all I found on our colonized seashore: the old illusions and anger of youth were gone. They were all strangers. I had long ago lost the one within me who could have come up with questions and enthusiasms.

Then there was the final pilgrimage to the sea: there was no way out.

"What an amazing evening, doctor . . . really marvelous, just like the end of the world, only no one thought to warn us about it! I can't get enough of gazing at the sky, the stars, your beautiful white hair, that aquiline nose with which you defy our world of dwarfish and frivolous prisoners."

Later he took leave of the doctor and walked away with a firm and even step, not showing the least sign of hesitation or confusion. He caught the first bus and changed at the university to another for the railroad station, where he enquired about trains to the seashore. He was told he'd have to wait seven hours: the season was over, and the next train would not leave until early in the morning.

He didn't feel like waiting that long on the cold empty platform of the desolate station. He should go home to bed, get up early in the morning: by then, most likely, the impulse would have died.

He took a few idle turns around the station, reluctant to abandon his idea. Then came the need to talk to someone. He walked to a telephone booth, stood there for a while, indecisive, orphaned. He thought he could remember the number . . . he started dialing.

He wanted to call the beautiful woman with whom he had lived through the period of his shaky return to reality, the return to a suspended life, to his ruminations. So many years had passed, so much fear, deception, submission, terror, drugs, more fear, questions, arguments, confusion, boredom, insomnia . . . Impossible to foresee, or to understand any of it. I've told you so much, Nana, and you found it all quite unbelievable. You sponged my forehead like a child's, you promised to take me by the hand and lead me to the warm and wonderful heart of reality. But my hands shook, weary, even then. But I did fight, remember, one, three, four, like some young sea lion, I fought, the waves didn't vanquish me, I knew how to survive. I came through, you were a witness, in spite of the raging inferno over my head. One, three, four . . . that's it, and then came the time of the so-called normalization, the reconciliation, the readjustment. A tarnished, shabby maturity, without enthusiasm, without hope or tragedies. Rules, laws, medications, taxes, dead ends, headaches. That's it, two, four, eight, that's got to be the number, multiply by two . . . two, four, eight, yes.

He hung up, retrieved the coin, redialed the number slowly and very carefully. I want to tell you things, Nana, yes I do. After you left, or is it after I chased you away . . . crooks, big-mouth con men, godfathers and godmothers, pimps and middlemen infested the earth. What a parade of them, hustlers, snake charmers, miracle workers. One, three, two, four, eight, I'm about to hear the voice of a warm and beautiful woman, an artist whom I nicknamed Nana, Nana Mouskouri, delicate and lovely, with her big romantic glasses. Oh my Nana, the rules, the fines, the denunciations, the marches, the patriotic hymns and the hypocrites have multiplied, but you have remained the same, Nana, with your interplanetary fee that poor televiewers of my ilk can no longer pay.

He heard the long, shrill sound, once, twice. Maybe she no longer existed, had been gone for a long time, that Sultana Manana Sorana or whatever the name was of that young tender and tenacious woman, so ready to save and shelter me in her heart that she kept embellishing with watercolors and gouaches. Sweet temptation, sultry voice . . . here she awakens, in a mist, from the frame of a long-lost, long-dead portrait.

Finally someone picked up the receiver. A woman's voice, hesitant, tentative. The night had sharpened the sound. He could sense surprise, emotion. But their conversations soon became halting, punctuated by restrained silences. The nocturnal drunken troubadour wasn't able to convince her of the importance of an immediate departure for the seashore. After a while he realized that it was indeed late, that she was tired, and also, it seemed, embarrassed by the presence of another person by her side. Yes, it seemed that there was someone else in the room. What do you expect, time goes by, people can't go on waiting forever, especially not their kind, the artists, highly strung and frail.

They didn't say much to one another. They didn't get to the

memory of his drowning, nor did they exchange intimate news about what had befallen them later, did not mention afflictions of skin and character. They remained wary and confused, as if they hadn't really recognized each other, or as if he'd happened to call some stranger who didn't have the heart to cut short the pleading of a voice that came out of the unknown, sounding hurt and childlike, at this hour.

The only concrete detail she seemed to convey was the fact that she'd seen a very relaxing movie that evening, in a down-town cinema. Relaxing, he repeated . . . and managed to keep her on the line. Relaxing . . . indeed, since she accepted the prolongation of this bizarre interruption of the nocturnal truce between two daylights. But "relaxing," how could it be that Nana had gotten used to such expressions, she who . . .

He stopped insisting on the travel plan but made her promise that she would go see the movie again with him the following evening.

What made it easier for him to conclude the conversation, and even took the edge off his disappointment, was the unex-pected pleasure of hearing the word "cinema." He had forgot-ten that word! How long had it been since he'd last seen a film? Evidently there still were cinemas, people standing in line, then politely taking their seats to enjoy the show. This bit of news calmed him instantly, magically banishing the exaggerated state of agitation in which he'd found himself for so many hours. The next day he didn't go to work but lazed around and indulged in meticulous preparations for the rendezvous.

But Nana didn't show up. He went in by himself, sat down, the movie began. It didn't take long for him to be enthralled by the comedy. He laughed in loud bursts, couldn't help himself. How long had it been since he had forgotten to laugh? He didn't have either a moment or the strength to stop. Tears were rolling down his cheeks, he couldn't help but whinny like a horse or a madman. The others around him complained in vain; he couldn't help himself.

All of his deteriorated organs seemed to shake in the spasms of that frantic crisis of merriment. After a while he felt real pain, he couldn't take it anymore.

He left the cinema half an hour before the end of the film. It was pretty outside. He looked at the street, much calmer now. He smiled, remembering some particularly funny scenes. The pain persisted; he even felt somewhat nauseated. The claw had dug deep into his chest, and he clutched himself. He felt a sharp stab that cut off his breath. He bent over, stricken, and held on for a few moments to the wrought-iron gate of the district court building, his head pulled between his shoulders, a somber expression on his face. His heart had suddenly become very fragile; suddenly, it couldn't resist any longer.

After that evening, the pain became stable but returned at regular intervals. With the infallibility of a metronome the symptoms kept warning him, and the schedule of his days was now marked by the syncopes of his agitated and fragile pulse.

PORTRAIT OF
THE YELLOW
APRICOT TREE

The break had been going on for who knows how long; time was passing by unchecked. The men opened their notebooks, leafed through them noiselessly, shifted their behinds on the school benches, sharpened their pencils or cleaned their pens. A faint rustling could barely be heard. The sunlight cascaded evenly. It was as if, though changing, everything had frozen in place, in an even gray mist.

The gestures seemed the same, familiar. Only the fear seemed to have lost its vigor; it had become more humble, slowing down the movements.

They were all wearing identical shiny black suits. Laundered shirts, glistening white, with stiff collars pinched together by the sharp triangle of a tie. Some were bald, some had become paunchy. There was the glitter of an occasional medal, of rings on fingers, of a blond beard.

But they'd retained something . . . the smile on a flaccid cheek, a movement, a greeting . . . since they had spotted me and were happy to see me again, they sent friendly signals my way.

Sleep had immersed me in the old classroom. I didn't know for how long I had been looking at their faces, at their hands, at their suits. I didn't dare check whether my hands had become as large as theirs, nor touch my suit or feel my tie to see whether they were the same too.

But there wasn't time, because the written examination was about to begin; they too should have been as terrified as in the past. And maybe they really were . . . some were rolling up tiny crib sheets and tucking them into their shoes. One, I noticed, had hid his in a crack in the bench. It was probably Rednik, unrecognizable now behind those incredibly thick glasses, were it not for the usual inkstains on his hands, and on his trousers too.

Many had unbuttoned their jackets—you could even see their suspenders! Those sweating more profusely had loosened their collars and ties. One kept nervously twisting the ring on his finger. The huge fellow by the hat rack was relentlessly opening and shutting a thin gilt cigarette case: it might have been Grigore, grown fat beyond measure and still sickly, because he was wearing, you could see it under his jacket, the same thick wool sweater. So they could still be recognized, even though they had become fat and weary, squeezed inside the elegant carcasses of their black suits.

Perhaps at least some of these family men had not forgotten the dreaded eve of the written examinations, the broken sleep, the nights of fear, the afternoons before the execution. Surely others also saw suddenly appear before them the specter of the one who corrected our untidy writing, our jumbled sums, with his long skinny arms. It was pointless to turn the page; he would appear on the next one too, and the next, even on the cover. I could not get rid of him even when I cast aside the notebook, even when I buried my nose in the algebra book, and later the trigonometry book. . . . He turned up everywhere, always the same pale figure, heavy-lidded, glued to the edge of the black-board in his usual posture, observing the hostile rows before him. He was no longer allowed to strike us. The year we first knew him—the first year of high school—the brutalities that calmed him had been forbidden. He tolerated us, we felt, with more and more difficulty, and with the same doggedness with which he tortured us. Our terror was as intense as his tolerance.

He would clench the fingers of his right hand around his belt as if they were claws. The belt seemed ready to pounce on us from the page of a textbook or a notebook, like a snake, to bloody our guilty faces.

At times he was able to satisfy his fury on a group of five or six. Other times he erupted when no one expected it, and I couldn't tell whether he was shouting at me or if he was already on to someone else. I could see myself being pushed back among the dumb ones at the back of the class, tumbling with every new setback, making way for the next, falling lower and lower, into the abyss, losing my voice, my wits, the strength to rise again.

I had come back to see them; I was, in fact, among those sitting in the rear. But my colleagues did not seem in the mood for jokes and horseplay. It seemed that they would no longer put up with the disapproval and contempt reserved for those who stayed back. Their profiles and their faces had become set, imperturbable. Their features had carved out a slightly somnolent, hermetic dignity. Very likely, maturity had taught them to deal with complications. In any event, they appeared far readier than in the old days for any contingency. Even for the one awaiting us.

They pretended to have forgotten the character walking between the rows of desks, stopping at the shoulder of one suspect or other.

Better to be like those who understood immediately, once

the questions were announced, that they did not stand a chance, and proceeded to fill their notebooks with any kind of nonsense.

Sometimes he seemed to catch on to the game. You could sense him smiling, about to explode; a spark would have been enough. You would have every reason to feel gratified if you imagined him alone in his room with the memory of your provocation.

I could not figure out which of the gentlemen around me would still have been capable of such a feat. I did not have time to examine each one; the bell was ringing. The sound had not perturbed them; they simply consulted their watches. They had straightened their backs and were waiting in a pregnant, icy calm. Did I also have a watch? I could not lift my arm, I seemed to be inside a dense cloud that oppressed and hampered my movements. There was a gigantic sneeze. I waited for the inevitable laughter to break out. Of course, everyone had recognized Lăzăroaie's trumpet; he was dying of fear as well. But no one batted an eyelid this time.

Then we all found ourselves standing. The door had opened, I dreamed; we had gotten up, I believe, then sat down again. Each one of us placed his notebook in front of him; no one raised an eye. He had thrown his briefcase soundlessly on his desk. He had turned toward us. I had the courage to glance up at him. He seemed paler and—a true miracle, a real coup!—he had smiled. Everything was suspended, along with us, but the light had become more intense, as had the whiteness of the walls, the windows.

They had probably felt the change too. They had lifted their heads, they saw him, but they did not seem frightened by the gash that the benevolent grimace had opened in his pale mask.

The dream had dressed them correctly. The worthy bureaucrats and family men did not notice that he wasn't wearing the clothes he used to. The dingy gray outfit that had flapped continually about his emaciated body was now replaced by a greenish uniform, closed at the neck. Small military lapels transversed by black stripes, the jacket pulled in at the waist by a wide belt. The boots were knee-high, and over them billowed the pleats of carefully pressed trousers.

The jacket in particular fitted him to perfection. And the narrow, shiny boots also showed off his litheness, his flexible, razor sharpness. They looked at him, bewildered. They could no longer hide behind their old school uniforms, nor could they find the right gestures, now that he too no longer hid behind the rags of the familiar suit, but had revealed himself in all his true and grand splendor, stiff and regal.

The funereal atmosphere of the classroom during the math assignment prevented them from being taken unawares and distracted by so many surprises. Taking advantage of this, they hunched, concentrated, over their notebooks. The head in front of me showed discoloration, and I realized that Mr. Bianu dyed his hair to keep it black and shiny, the way it used to be. At the blackboard, the sentry stood waiting for us to copy the examination paper's title.

He had forgotten to assign us as many subjects as there were rows of students, as was his custom. Across the entire width of the board, in orange chalk and with big round letters, he had written a single theme for us all. He then stepped to one side so as not to obstruct our view.

They bent over their notebooks, immobile: the dream had frozen. They looked at the blank pages as if in a daze; perhaps they would never come to life again, but the light became steadily clearer, as did the air in the room, purer and purer. A delicate and agreeable breeze touched every forehead. They lifted their eyes again, rejuvenated and serene, and smiled at him. But he had turned his back, he didn't see them anymore.

He was always blocking some section of the blackboard with his narrow body, and especially with the rapid movements of his long arms. With one hand he wrote, with the other he erased and corrected. He kept covering the black screen with colored symbols, always different ones, which I only became aware of, without understanding them, when he shifted from one end of the blackboard to the other.

The silence lasted for quite some time. I followed the movement of his arms into a box of multicolored chalks and into another box, much larger, filled with colored clay, bits of which he kneaded a little between his fingers before applying to the board. The blackboard became more and more colorful, alive with red and brown and green spots, dusty areas burned by the sun.

One could hear the sound of laughter, weak at first, then growing louder and louder; it was the first time that something like that had happened. Bursts of laughter, whispers, rattling, whistling. But if you turned toward the class you would have seen nothing. The rows were perfectly aligned, the dutiful, respectable gentlemen staring with big, frozen eyes either at the board or at their notebooks.

I thought I heard a squeak of laughter nearby. I looked at my neighbor. Black suit, tie, shirt like the others. A shiny gold-plated pen. A small, sharp, mouselike face, with pockmarked skin. Things were coming back to me, but here was one I did not recognize. His hair was completely white, and he had small, well-looked-after hands. He was missing a finger on his right hand. He was smiling too, a kind smile, guilty. He pointed his hand toward the cigarettes beside his notebook. Friendly, shy gestures. The look of a nice man. He was repeating the offer when I caught sight of the same title, transcribed on the first page of his notebook. His handwriting was messy, with tall, spiky, cuneiform letters. But he had copied correctly from the blackboard: PORTRAIT OF THE APRICOT TREE.

The noise had grown to a veritable tumult. I did and I did not hear it. It seemed that they had even begun to push the desks around. A happy pandemonium possessed them all. I would have turned to catch them in the act, wild and riotous, had I not known that they would have stopped dead the moment I laid eyes on them.

But it was not necessary anyway, because something else had interrupted them. The revolt died down, you couldn't hear a sound. Something around us had changed again. The air, the light, had become rarefied. I too felt the breeze, a waft of fresh air.

In effect, the windows had opened of their own accord: the air that was drifting in was scented, cooler, a little humid. I was able to look at them. They seemed surprised, subdued, timid, their brows refreshed by the breeze.

I saw him again too, by the blackboard, as at the beginning, standing in his jungle cat's uniform.

We remained in front of him only a moment, no longer. We were shrinking into enraptured, silly schoolchildren. A long, inaudible cry of pleasure welled up within us. The same gratified smile appeared on the large, flaccid faces of the functionaries.

Only then did I feel a closeness to them. Something sweet and fresh was enveloping us.

The landscape on the board had expanded into a bizarre relief of dark, clayey soils; of gentle hills covered in green, sparkling moss; of small pine trees on which hung pointed, coffee-colored cones that bombed the resplendent green-grass sea.

We had come back to life, enraptured by the unfolding view, by the new fragrance of the forest.

His hunter's or perhaps woodsman's uniform and the pallor

that lengthened and sharpened his features no longer seemed to frighten the ex-students; they had grown used to them. They were participating, I felt, as eagerly as I was in the convenient surprise provided by the landscape. He observed them tenderly, with a restrained, worn-out hatred, with a sort of welcome, in fact. I could hear around me the hushed rustling of their stealthy, unsure gestures, the intermittent words, a cry of joy, gentle breathing, as in the past; the indolent bustling, the impatience of an agitated ant-hill; small squeaks of pleasure, soothed panic, and the care taken to temper violent outbursts lest the fairy-tale spell be broken. Indeed, any rash imprudence might have ripped the film that moistened our eyes.

An inexplicable, fearful nervousness, however, lent a brittle quality to the wait. The windows were dripping, licked by long veins of water.

The glass itself seemed to have become liquid, evaporating in the light, cool fog that had made our clothes feel less heavy, that had tinted the benches and the walls, rocking us. We were lost in a cloud of floral giddiness. A sunny, complete liberation.

I could no longer see my distinguished colleagues. With a grinding effort I managed to unscrew myself from the spot in which I had remained petrified.

Using all my strength, I turned abruptly toward them. The air had somehow become a fog of fine ash, yellowish-red, purplish, or golden, I don't know, it was like a vaporous smoke, occluding vision. I could barely make them out, crowded together, enveloped in the distance. In the corner of the classroom I succeeded in distinguishing the three majestic trees, the coat racks, on which the hats of the distinguished gentlemen dangled like melons, because the light had changed little by little to a pale, sickly green that was blurring the edges of everything.

My schoolmates were wriggling about somewhere, their

tumbling and the field at times seemed just a step away. Their neckties had come loose, they were flapping, as were their jackets with the long vents at the back. Sparkles of cufflinks and medals. One could hear a whisper, a muffled panting. The grass was charged with strange currents that sparked at the slightest touch. Blades of grass chased around their hairy nostrils, toward the large, red ears. Wreaths of flames pushed forth continuously at the mere contact with the hair on the hands or with the mustache of some bureaucrat or other. And then they would disappear once again, swallowed up by the landscape.

I turned, exhausted, toward my neighbor. I no longer could see even him clearly. Only his grown-up face flushed with contentment. He was crunching on candy; he offered me his bag full of sweets, red and round, small, sticky bombs. He belched with gusto, radiant with uncontainable joy. He had spread his arms wide to show me the dozens of photographs lined up on his desk. They were pictures of a child in every conceivable position and at every conceivable age. They were of his son, or perhaps of himself as a child; but our breathing kept fogging up the prints. The ecstasy bore him away, too quickly, and I lost sight of him.

I managed to remember the notebook, to retrieve the words that were written there. The others kept slipping away, remote, into the tunnels of the forest, on the thin wind that ruffled their hair. I tried to tear myself away from the vertiginous fragrances and colors. I wanted to discover, standing out in relief on the blackboard, the apricot tree.

For a long moment I could discern no more than hills of cracked clay, small lichen islands, the distorted reflection of the tall grass that tangled itself against the shoulders of trees weeping tears of sap. Dry acorns, old, grayish pine cones . . . The landscape seemed gradually to be giving itself up to dusk.

A fine, silting powder of purplish chalk was coming down,

then the darkness. I still succeeded in making out, down toward the right, below the rim of a dune, some yellowish marks and thin reddish stripes, perhaps the place of the apricot tree. The stillness was not merely silence. A whispering murmur of calm, cold waters. A perfect, total peace. The petals opened and closed, vibrant, like the air that silently rocked the spiny branches of the pines. Light, shiny missiles flew through the air; you could hear the hail of fresh fruit as it pelted us.

For an instant I felt their hot down caress my face; my mouth was filled with freshness. But I knew that in reality I was different, heavier and older, tortured by other dreams in which the trials of the past were revived, overturning my age and keeping me from becoming a grown man; but now my body and my mind had become clearer; I felt young, alive, happy, and I didn't want it to end. It rained luminous apricots, small golden balls, the branches arched and sprang back, whipping the air. I saw the vault of the sky—spherical, azure calm. How they once had dragged, those suddenly all-too-short afternoons before the examinations, the executions. You hardly knew how to pass the time. All the courtyards were empty; refusing rest and nourishment, I would steal among the gray clouds where phantoms lurked and the vitreous dome of night had ballooned.

The apricot tree had revealed itself once more; again there were the reassuring yellow circles that lit the sky with the gold of firm, dense fruit. As I ventured into the depths of the blackboard, the relief opened up protectively with a murmur of invisible waters that cooled my brow.

I was more and more alone; my distinguished colleagues had disappeared. I could not find a trace of the agitation of the schoolboys. I was lost, mad with delight. I wanted to dance for joy, hysterical, I wanted to see them, reanimate that foolish intoxication of the past, out of whose grinning mouth we tumbled, little cannibals squeezed into tight suits and throttled by ties that burned like torches. But I was slumbering in a gentle exhaustion I had never experienced before. Serene and alone, I filled the entire notebook, open to the page that bore the colored chalk imprint of a big, wrinkled hand.

The evening wind burned my lips and brow. Barbarous sunsets, facing the barracks, before the executions, the examinations. . . . So he had reappeared, hands smudged with red and all other colors of chalk, walking down the rows of the condemned. He was snarling with that same indulgence and holding his palms high so as not to soil his uniform. He was coming closer, I could feel it; he had taken the first step.

Fear seized me again, encircled me, whirled me to the surface. But the enchantment had not abandoned me yet, the waves were receding without haste. Sleep was ebbing, though it still had me and my eyes in its embrace.

He approached slowly, almost imperceptively. I was shaking; the wait exhausted me, disturbed me. Now he drew near and stroked my hair gently. He wiped the last traces of color on my head, then lowered his heavy hand; I felt it on my arm. As if he had chosen me, as if he were announcing my destiny.

I could not move. He was shaking me carefully by both shoulders, but I was transfixed, I did not move. I could not free myself of the apricot tree, of the sky laden with fruit and leaves, of the peace of deserted afternoons, of the childish trembling, as if I were delirious. Familiar words would move closer, I could sense it.

The magic, the fear, the sun of the apricot tree, the protective silence of trees, the soft, golden clay, would have endured, just as before. . . . The hand slid down my brow, toward my neck, on my shoulders, inside my damp shirt, on my thin, frail bones. Incredibly, I was grown, like my colleagues! They too had lost their parents; they could no longer have understood or treasured the wonder, the sickness, the exhaustion of so splendid a night, a night from which I should have awakened a grown, healed man.

He was shaking me, but I could not get up. I was trying with all my strength to gain some time, to put off the moment. . . .

THE PARTITION

THE ONSLAUGHT of early-morning streetcars . . . purple rectangles of the window. His head tries to rise an inch: a throttled groan in the pillow. Vibration of the balcony, rumbling brontosaurs crushing the train tracks. His body shudders in the shelter of eiderdown. Next door a radio is switched on. Sometimes, not often, the phone . . . a quarter of an hour . . . the Yale key in the lock and then nothing, no one. In the afternoon the telephone starts ringing. The crisp voice always seems so fresh, so energetic. Radio, TV, guests dropping by. Melancholy nights, recordings of cellos and guitars.

At dawn the metallic hordes once more on the offensive. His body jumps, falls back again. Purple windows, tormented half-sleep. And again, morning waltzes on the radio, news briefs, a chair—bang—is slid back, a key—click—is turned in the lock.

"The tenants on your floor are all good people. The Zaharescu family, no problems. The apartment opposite the staircase is shared by the priest, the woman lawyer, and the gym teacher. Next door is the officer with his gaggle of children, the engineer and his lawyer wife, the tailor, and the bookkeeper, you know, the woman with the pockmarked face. Across the way is Bratu, poor old Bratu, the dentist. And then right next to you there's Mrs. Cornelia. Yes, well, you can't say that she's had much luck in her life. . . ."

The building superintendent: thick-set, punctual, hygienic. Hairy, swarthy. The eyes of a makeshift expert. A conversationalist by profession. At 7:00 A.M. he's at his post in the lobby. At 10:00 P.M. he locks the metal front gate. Any unfamiliar face is noticed immediately. Visitors must explain everything: whose place, for what reason, for how long. With all these drifters hanging around, thieves, provocateurs, we have to stay alert.

Indeed he is alert, tirelessly so. He asks questions, takes notes, remembers, registers. The tenants greet him with respect and caution. A caretaker, a responsible man, very responsible, there's no denying it . . . he keeps an eye on the upkeep of the building, the hot water and central heating, the keys to the mailboxes, the elevator, the garbage, the bulletin board, the rents. The tenant list, the registration of foreigners, the maintenance file are completely up to date. He's obliging, too, always ready to help install a TV antenna, change a gas canister, fix a telephone, a broken lock, venetian blinds, replace floorboards, stop a leaky faucet, move furniture. Attentive to everything—no chance of being surprised by the unforeseen—he examines, watches, checks every apartment. Ask him in for coffee and he'll refuse, but drop by to pay your monthly rent and he's glad to keep the conversation going.

"So you had your share of difficulties, it seems, before you moved in here. Yeah, your apartment there was pretty, uh . . . an apartment that caught the eye of . . . who knows who . . . and suddenly . . . But don't worry, you'll be okay here. . . . Say, I meant to ask you, I never did get the whole story . . . it seems that you're out of work at the moment."

The explanations made seem confused to him; he senses a delicate situation. So he learns when you were born, where you studied. "Ah, I wanted to tell you, the priest across the way there, you know, and the old lawyer, well, sometimes they peep through keyholes, so watch it. The Zaharescus are okay.

Though you have to admit they've got enough problems of their own, too, what with their daughter who stayed in Austria. They lost everything, can you imagine, at their age, and her their only child, too. And Mrs. Cornelia, not much luck with her either, poor woman; her husband emigrated, so you understand, what do you expect her to do . . . you must have heard of her. That's right, she was an actress before. Now she works at the National Tourism Office."

He loves these confidences, but he won't press you.

Streetcar-tanks rattle the ashen windows in the early morning. Workers drag themselves painfully out of bed, reeling with sleep. Bathroom, kitchen, coat rack in the hall . . . a stampede to the elevator, down the staircase. The streetcar stops directly under his window. Suddenly the huddled groups of bodies break up. Arms stretch up, dozens of gloved hands reach out to clasp cold damp bars on dirty doors. Squeezed in among coats, briefcases, umbrellas, the lady's checked cape is crushed and its lining makes a funny grating sound. She keeps tossing back her long blond hair, but the crush of the crowd abbreviates the gesture. Ejected from the streetcar—just in time—in front of the NTO offices, she stands still for a moment on the sidewalk, dazed, then straightens her clothes. . . .

The chair, hello hello, smile, the boss, a little coffee, pretty good that one, you heard the latest, ring ring, Sunday's baptism, the hard currency collection plan, folk choir practice; appointment, rally, meeting, political instruction, quarterly evaluation, recipe for baklava, paramilitary training session, beauty salon, certification of professional and ideological aptitude. Oh, the worker's days! Messages from the switchboard, ring ring, orders to pass along, a bit more coffee, and have you heard this one, the boss's ties, gossip, newspapers, brochures, summons to political meetings, fashion magazine, report to make, cutbacks, not wasting office supplies . . . corner to hide in, handshake, the little flirtation, a wink, ready-made answers, a bottle of aspirin, mascara, imported nylons, the monthly payment on the gas heater.

At some point they wake up, hurry, leave, rush around like greyhounds; flee from the rat race; their eyes emtpy, they scatter in the streets toward shops, trams, the bus. Lines for cheese, medication, flashlights, buttons, TV sets. A line here, another there: books, light bulbs, padlocks, shoes, eyeglasses, and so on until nightfall. Twilight eases their exhaustion. Up the staircase of standardized buildings, concrete boxes, the leftover hours pass lazily: armchair, TV, gas heater, ironing, the nightly sarcophagus.

In the lobby the superintendent receives the greetings of his flock. He answers each one with a light nod. Always attentive, he notes, makes out, identifies your shopping bag, packages, voice, clothes, who you're with. The rhythm of your steps, any hesitation, the least trace of bad humor, everything is recorded. Such an important building, such different people, in short the community demands its own laws: to know everyone, ward off conflict, to inform correctly, make judicious decisions, have one's eye on everything. At one time he lived in a maid's room and worked at a warehouse, but he got into some sort of trouble, there was a trial, prison. Later—rehabilitation, work, punctuality, irreproachable behavior. A studio apartment, a superintendent. A portly man, neat, perfectly disciplined.

Food shopping, the hours at the office, the manager's eager scrutiny, the morning's events at the NTO . . . The full report is available half an hour after the neighbor gets home. "But no, listen, I'm no longer qualified to be even a second-rate paper pusher in that shitty office, and all because of my husband, the 'absentee.' Relatives living abroad, come on! When they kicked me out of the theater I explained at the trial that I hadn't done anything. I couldn't know what he was going to do. Good Lord, what do they want from me? They fired the man who was director then . . . what more do they want? They hung that story on me like a string of old pots and now I'll drag it around for the rest of my life. Of course I'm nervous! I spent the hours running from store to store, but there's nothing, nothing. It's Mother's birthday Saturday—how am I going to bake her a cake? . . . TV? What TV? Don't you see that they . . . which newscast? No, I don't know anything, I wasn't listening. That may be so, but what does it have to do with me?"

At night the street noises subside. Soft, muffled throbbing. The city recedes, the concrete boxes float in a haze of exhaustion. Once in a while the neighbor strains her ears for signs of the gentleman next door. Nothing. Never anything. Must be an old quadriplegic or a deaf-mute child. Once, when she was downstairs paying the rent, the superintendent asked her, "And how are you getting on with your neighbor, Comrade Cornelia?" "Comrade" Cornelia, what an ass! For years it had been nothing but "As madam says" here, "Madam is right" there. The information supplied by Comrade Superintendent about the fellow next door is not particularly disturbing: he hangs around all day, he has nothing to do with anyone in the building, he didn't even come to the tenants' meeting. Instead of doing his stretch of voluntary labor he chose to pay a twenty-leu fine and stayed home. The man has his problems, and screw everything else. But the superintendent must know everything about him, too. You know, it seems that people have seen him carrying a bundle of foreign magazines under his arm. "People"—who? The superintendent, of course, who else? Looks like he drinks, too. Where does he get his whiskey, I wonder? All you can find in town is tainted wine and wood alcohol. And the turtleneck sweaters . . . that's all he wears, you never see him dressed like everyone else, in a suit, with a shirt and tie. Only turtlenecks! They're all imported, you can tell it a mile away, he gets packages. He was asked to write about ethics and justice for the building's newsletter. "I said to him, you seem to be an educated man," the super recounted to me, but the man just hemmed and hawed and mumbled some sort of an excuse.

Once there had been no partitions. Old building, well built, huge apartments, rich people. Then they built partitions thin as cigarette paper, reallocated living space, redid everything. Bricks, you couldn't find one in these new partitions; they don't insulate and yet the acoustics are far from perfect. Simply annoying, that's all.

Newspapers, pills, albums, medicine bottles, books, pipes, envelopes, notebooks, knickknacks, old clothes, dictionaries: the cage of a flunked student! Furors and terrors, musty den: weekly weather reports, racetrack schedules, lists of things to do, a log of migraines. A cell, a patient, gloomy silence. As if he hadn't heard of death, as if he had all the time in the world.

She's not so far off the mark, his neighbor: the whole day he loafs around. The day amounts to this: articles, hours and hours, spleen and suspicion, a narrow band around which the calendar turns. The city slides into the black mud of night, phosphorescent shadows, army barracks. Cold, shame, terror, and nightmares, screams muffled in the pillow of darkness.

"Troubles and a migraine, that's all I've got, if you must know," the neighbor shouts at her unexpected visitor.

Late, the city drowning in night and oblivion.

"What are you doing here at this hour?" demands Comrade Cornelia. Still, one hears the sound of a key turning in the lock: the intruder has been let in.

"So? I don't have to account to anyone. No . . . to anyone. Don't touch me. You, my husband? You're joking. You're insane, let go of me! You want me to phone your wife? Get out of here . . . get lost! Fine, I'll call her . . . why should I wait?

That's what *you* think! You don't scare me, not even a big shot like you. So what more can they take away from me? All I have left is . . . And that's what you've come for, right? Dirty old beast." Blows deflected, whispers, shush-shush, silence.

At dawn the assault of columns of armored streetcars. The pillow, a wet paste, jumps, falls back with its load. Radio, telephone? Nothing. The Yale lock is silent. No signs.

Toward noon, music, faucet, shower, telephone. Her voice is warm, calm. "Sure I know them. . . . Ten hours in a row I'm glued to my chair, listening, always listening, I'm going crazy. The others, too. No one moves an inch, you'd think they were a bunch of recruits. . . . After that, what they . . . I hear there are going to be cuts in the staff. . . . No, it doesn't bother me. Go for a walk? Where? Haven't you seen what's going on in the streets? A restaurant? That tempts you? Two women alone? Bad and expensive, you know that. What music? Where? You know very well that everything's closed by ten. And the streets are as dark as pitch. . . . Oh, good, thank you. Oh if you could, it would be wonderful! Three hundred grams, yes, for Mother's cake. Okay, I'll come by, of course. . . . If it makes me happy . . . sure . . . I'm not made of stone. Yes, that's it. . . . If I could squeeze into a mouse hole . . . just to sleep, that's all. Yes, yes, they destroyed us. Sleep, forget everything. . . . Yes, I'll be there, I promise."

At one the early news reports. . . . Someone rang the doorbell. Ding-a-ling, the little music box. Ding-a-ling. Wait a minute, it isn't the neighbor's. . . . All these bells ring alike. The door opens. On the threshold, his neighbor! At last one sees her: fortyish, face still young, lovely hair, good figure. The gentleman is a bit sleepy; as he opens the door he is buttoning up his thick blue shirt, which hangs over old, shabby jeans.

"You must have left something on the stove. . . . I smell burning."

She smiles, protective. A warm voice, but potentially high, even shrill. She runs her hand through her hair, a little disconcerted by the man's scrutiny. What an absentminded fellow!

"Yes, I guess I'm guilty." He tries to grin boyishly. A step backward.

Should he ask her in? There would be no point, there's an adolescent's mess in an old man's room. First he should rush into the kitchen. . . . He runs, pushes off the scorched pot, opens the window . . . the smell . . . he takes a rag, grabs the pot again, drops it in the sink, turns on the faucet, fsshhit, fsshhit, the water sizzles, steam rises, the smell of burning.

The front door was left ajar, but she is gone again. No time even to thank her, to apologize. . . . He could always ring her doorbell, what he'd heard last night would be a good excuse; yes, afterward, that would risk . . . especially being next-door neighbors.

The superintendent is at his post in the lobby.

"I haven't seen you in a while! You hardly ever leave your room. It makes one wonder what you eat—I've never seen you at the grocery store either. You're a bit secretive, comrade. Oh, don't take it badly, I didn't mean it, I was joking! The other tenants keep asking me, I never know what to tell them. By the way, I've got a letter for you."

He had the envelope ready in his pocket, in case the strange fellow should decide, eventually, to leave his lair. He'd have to pass through the lobby, and there, at his post . . .

"From Brazil! Ah, you have pretty wide connections," the superintendent mutters, frustrated that the oddball had quickly shoved the letter into his pocket without even looking at it. "No, don't worry about the rent. When you have a moment, just come by and we'll settle it." But the fellow, intimidated, had already sneaked off toward the exit.

Out in the street the loudspeakers are wailing: Hurray! Hur-

ray! At the tobacco shop a pleasant surprise: no line. Pale and
tousled, the saleslady is knitting.

"Matches? We don't have any. Haven't had any in two
weeks." Now he doesn't have the courage to bother her any
further. Finally he dares, with polite formulas: "Would you be
so kind . . . I would appreciate . . ." The saleslady is not easily
impressed, but neither is she foul-tempered. She is used to the
naiveté of people always asking for this or that and a thousand
other things she doesn't have; all she can offer is correct information.

"Chinese cigarettes? You're dreaming! No Chinese or Bulgarian cigarettes since last spring. I still have two packs of
Admiral. Take them both now, my friend. You won't see any
more soon." No sense being offended by her familiarity. A
friendly gesture, the proof was the two packs—a rarity.

A few cautious steps to the door of his building. For once the
superintendent is not there. He's probably in the boiler room
or at the incinerator, unless someone called him to talk over
payments or a lease. Quick, quick, the suspect makes a dash for
the elevator and presses the button. He looks around. Impatient, he starts up the stairs, taking two, three steps at a time.
Whew, he made it! He rummages in his pockets for his key,
can't find it. Ah, here it is, in his pants pocket. . . .

"Ah, back so soon?"

His voice! But where is it coming from? By the elevator, the
door of the communal apartment is open. The retired lawyer
is smiling beatifically at the superintendent. So, the neighbor
across the way is having some problems. No chance of closing
that door; she is planted there, above all she won't miss this.

"I forgot to tell you, pal," continues he-who-knows-all, "the
mailman left a package with all kinds of magazines for you.
Come get it, I've had it for several days now."

But how could the mailman have given it to him, I've only

been out for . . . He's not allowed to hand it over to anyone else. How could he . . . The tenant would like to argue, but he can't. He drags himself, sweating, behind the always ame-nable superintendent. The son of a bitch! He's in no hurry, no, he's got all the time in the world! But I won't go into his apartment, he won't get anything out of me. I'll stand in the doorway, all he has to do is hand over what he is supposed to, a package, a bomb, a summons, a prison sentence, what-ever he wants.

And so the man remains on the threshold of the studio apartment. No desire, none, to look at the pastel walls, the perfect symmetry of the knickknacks, the pinups, the thick carpet, the leather armchair, the stereo. The superintendent brings him a roll of magazines bound in a yellow sleeve.

"I can see your friends take good care of you! Great! Friends like that, anytime . . . Brazil, France, Canada, Belgium. Always plenty for you to read. It would be nice if you could lend them to me. . . . Once you've read them, of course, when you're done with them. Instead of throwing them out. . . . I could thumb through them in the evening . . . helps pass the time."

But what's got into them all today, why are they so familiar? Must be my fault, there must be something about me that brings it out. First "Mr." here, "Mr." there, then bam! "It would be nice if you could lend them to me." As if he hadn't looked through them already. He hadn't kept them all this time for nothing. From Canada, Belgium . . . no, this one's from Marseilles. The letter, you've examined it, yes, that one came from Brazil. But when did you ever see me get mail from Canada and Belgium? And you're saying that to make me think you know everything, can do anything. . . . Next you'll be asking me in for a cup of coffee, a cup of coffee today, another one tomorrow . . . and so on, until . . . until!

"You sure you won't come in? I'll make you a good cup of

coffee. I have real coffee, the real stuff. You're in a hurry? You never have time, never have time. . . ."

The solitary tenant managed to extricate the roll of magazines from the hands of the vigilant super, who was watching him, smiling. The tenant smiled, too, humbly, thanking the mustachioed, impeccable, deodorized, perfumed superintendent. . . . A calm, pleasant voice, and those tight-fitting, well-ironed pants with one cuff enclosed in a metal bicycle clip. Impeccable get-up, military bearing, master of all the rules, you can't fault him. . . . Brown-haired, rigid, inflexible: OK, you don't want to joke with us, recite us a little poem, wink at us once in a while. . . . Proud, secretive, but then you're not the only one with something to hide. . . . You're not very talkative, as if we're not quite . . . But you'll come around someday, you've got no choice, everyone does, you *have* to.

At the neighbor's a special radio program, prewar tangos. The windows are wet with rain. The music lover winds up the evening with Slavic music, a cello piece. Wrapped up in his warm blanket, it's hot, soft, like when he was a child.

The tram drivers: schoolchildren in uniform. The passengers: kids. The traffic policemen: elementary-school children. The saleslady at the tobacco stand: a little girl with tresses. And the superintendent, yes, him, none other than the pimply-faced tattletale in fifth grade. We get to school on time, the bell, a line for class, backs straight, arms folded on the desks. Uniforms, recess. We're good, we drink our glass of milk. We get out of school, it's already dusk, we go buy notebooks, pencils, we redeem tickets for bread and margarine. At home we quickly close the window to shut out the roar of the armored cars. We no longer hear the athletes in ranks marching in cadence, ceaselessly, one two, one two, from morning till night.

The streets are humming, fights everywhere, a shop window explodes, they beat up some guy who helped himself to two portions at a restaurant and the lazy oaf who was late opening his store. Brawlers do as they please, they stop anyone they want, "Hey you there, yeah you, where's your school?" And bam!—punched when you least expect it. Order, good Lord, there must be order, the schoolchildren are well-behaved but terrified anyway, and disorder grows, amplifies. Hey, that guy grabbed me for no reason, I have a ticket, I swear, I can show it to you. He pulls me by the ears, makes me get off, he shoves me, pushes me against a dirty wall in a dark alley where no one can see us. "Guys like you, I know you . . . get that into your head. You better be scared, you hear? And I'll protect you. But don't try to hide anymore, got it?" He shoves a large envelope covered with stamps under my nose. He doesn't have an unpleasant voice, this pimply snitch from the fifth grade, but he yells too loudly, he's too sure of himself. "And where do you get your chow, huh? Tell me, you little louse. . . . You better be really hungry, you hear? I'll give you what you need, but first you gotta learn, see? I'll teach you right. In ten years I'll have made a man of you." He pulls me by my ears, brings his long pimply face close to mine, his eyes bulging. "Ten years from now you'll do what you're told. I'll take care of you, you little worm. But never hide anything from me, understand? I'll answer for you. You'll see how well I'll get you into shape. You'll come as soon as I whistle, I tell you. And hey, you'll do well." He searches for the whistle in his vest pocket, doesn't find it, shoves two fingers in his mouth, lets out a long, strident whistle. Young hoodlums appear from every corner of the square, ready to tear me to pieces. . . .

The neighbor wakes up sweating, his nose buried in his pillow. He stretches out his hand toward the bedside lamp, can't find it, panics. He reaches out again, presses the switch. Unfamiliar room, cold. Where am I? He curls up, counts, one, two . . . five, turns out the light. Pulls the blanket over his head.

The grinder turns slowly, steadily. A gigantic piece of machinery. The spectators to whom it is being demonstrated are no bigger than beetles next to Gulliver's boot. Hundreds of them hang on the enormous crank, turning it and turning with it, up, down, up in a steady rhythm. The steel mouth spouts thick lumps of ground meat trickling a reddish juice. Some of the spectators in a circle beneath the mouth try to escape, but have to return, forbidden to leave; they must watch. They cover their eyes. Jets of bloody ground meat pour down on them; they throw up, run all over the place, horrified, come back, are transfixed. It's summer, the dog days, everyone is sweating. The demonstration takes place in a public square. Above the crowd, dozens of loudspeakers explain the operation, provide technical details, now and then bark sharp orders. The crank turns, turns, monotonously, the clusters of bodies hanging on it rising, dropping, multicolored scarabs clinging to the gleaming steel bar that reflects the sun. The ground meat spills out, long bowels of it breaking as they hit the ground. The spectators fall, vomit, climb out from the streams of flesh, tangles of ground meat and bodies mixing together, gathering in piles. . . .

The tenant wakes up again with a start, his heart in his throat. For a long time he hunches over the sink, then staggers back into his room, his face damp. He opens the window, welcomes the cold air. The dinosaurs are already rumbling on their tracks; the town begins to rise, still numb, from the mist of sleep. His neighbor is listening to military marches.

The tenant returns to the bathroom. Hurriedly he shaves, washes, gets dressed. From the back of his closet he digs out an old briefcase covered with dust, wipes it, puts on his coat, locks the door. In front of the elevator he runs into the gym teacher, a mild-mannered man with a blond crew cut. Hello, hello, they squeeze together in the narrow cubicle. Not a word during the descent, and on their faces the absent look of people counting floors until the ride is over. . . .

In the street, swarms of hurrying silhouettes. He melts into them, walks along the quay. People get to work, disappear inside, others replace them. He walks and walks, lost in thought, and finds himself alone somewhere in a distant part of town. He turns around and walks toward the center of town.

He steps into a gallery. How much are these? Depends on the size. Are landscapes cheaper than portraits? He goes by a closed synagogue, its doors boarded up. He waits in line among chattering old women, but they're told that the shop had run out of milk. He asks a traffic policeman what this neighborhood is called and how to get to the railroad station. Policemen all over the place, sometimes even groups of them, here and there. He joins another line; it would be good to get a few rolls of toilet paper, but there are too many people, it would take hours. He passes a church. Door open, a candle burning, no one inside, he waits for an hour, still no one, no priest, none of the faithful.

He is suddenly very hungry, but decides to ignore it. In a miserable square he sits on a bench from where he can see, through a window, the gym of a kindergarten. Bundled up in their uniforms, the children are lined up in pairs, practicing drills.

Rested now, he resumes his walk. When he reaches the entrance to a hospital some people are leaving and he tags along behind them. One woman in a green coat goes into a pastry shop. He follows her in and finds her seated at a little white marble table. A dozen or so plump pastries wrapped in waxed paper lie on a plate before her. Still young, pretty, very pale, her hair thick and long, shining. No, the question doesn't bother her. She answers calmly, in detail. She gives a sort of sociological essay, not always easy to follow. One feels ill at ease, she explains, because one feels excluded. . . . One can't

take responsibility, what can you do about it? Yesterday afternoon, for instance, I found the Cabaret Rousseau locked up,
and the comic opera is closed, too, ever since old da Vinci was
drafted into the reserves. And sir you can't go dancing anywhere, either. We once had dancing classes, dance halls everywhere, perhaps you remember that superb Leopardi, on
Griviţa Avenue . . . or Rosa, who danced only with her partner,
Karl de Luxembourg, I forget the address.

The tenant is back at the same time as the others, who, work
over, have slipped back into their cages. A large crowd at the
entrance to his building; no one is allowed in. On the threshold,
flanked by two policemen, the superintendent is checking iden-
tification papers. The tenant realizes that he has left his at
home. But yes, the pimply one can identify him: the superintendent reluctantly mumbles a confirmation. After a quarter of
an hour the tenant is allowed in. Well, you'd never have
guessed that she, that nuisance of a lawyer, would do herself in.
. . . Of course, when it comes to gas it's hard to tell, it could
have been an accident.

His neighbor joins him at the elevator. She looks tired, but
still young. Her beautiful hair, loose, catches the light. That
outfit with its little stiff collar suits her well, very well. Big green
eyes, smile, her lips moist. Just the two of them in the elevator.
Yes, it has to be endured. This dangerous intimacy provokes
her to break in, "You know, they've often asked me about you
. . . not just *him*, but others, too. Nothing serious, don't worry,
no. I told them you're very nice, a model neighbor. Quiet, no
visitors, never any noise. Nothing suspicious in that, is there?"
She has a large brown handbag on her shoulder, and a silk
scarf, burgundy, around her neck. She opens her handbag; on
her keys dangle tiny lucky charms. At her door she smiles again:
evening, *ciao*, bye.

In the end it's better to go out, like everybody else: you run

errands, it's nobody's business, to each his own. The tenant can
no longer bear to stay indoors. He leaves, going nowhere in
particular, out in the street, morning till night, for weeks on
end. He walks away months, seasons. Pharmacies, butcher
shops, movie theaters, restaurants, clothes shops, parks,
schools, clinics, garages, he comes to know them all. No one
can accuse him of staying cooped up in his room all by himself.
Now at least he knows the city like the back of his hand.

But eventually he is tired. So what, he'll take the risk, come
what may, again he'll coop himself up away from everyone.
Bizarre, but if anyone asked him he could certainly justify his
isolation. Still, it's probably best for everybody to leave things
be, no explanations. The place is a mess but comfortable, a
strongbox, a redoubt, an off-course space station that sometimes picks up signals marking the passage of time.

"Suit yourself, but you'll never set foot in my apartment
again. It's over . . . because it just is, that's all. It was late at
night, you took me by surprise. . . . Enough, I've got my own
life. I'm fed up. Yes, how about that, this is it, I've joined
. . . me too . . . yes, and it was unanimous. Why wouldn't they
have accepted me? The others, they don't have more principles
than me, but they're no worse, either, come on. Yeah, and they
all work like dogs, they've been there quite a while. . . ."

"I slipped him a hundred and still they kept her there for
four days without so much as taking her temperature!"

"Yes, thank you, of course I'll be there. How could one fail
to participate in something so important! Of course I'll alert
them. Oh, it's not hard, I'll tell them it's their responsibility,
otherwise they'll only have themselves to blame. . . ."

A light, golden autumn. Tender light, undulating, a ribbon
of rainbow. Pedestrians relax, undo the jacket of their uniforms, stop to contemplate the superb void of the sky.

The noises next door tell him that his neighbor is home, that she didn't go to work this morning. He goes downstairs and hides behind a pillar of the building across the street, watching for her, waiting.

Murky dawn, assault of the elephants, the screeching of the tracks, hordes of passersby, hours of emptiness and submission, jokes, frights, news, discipline, stale-tasting dishes, encounters, slogans, frustrations, elevator, TV, phone, and above all she is utterly dissatisfied, perfectly adapted, but more and more dissatisfied. She's not the same, it is not her, he has to see her. . . . But she didn't go out that day, unless he missed her. Over the next few days he takes up his post again, watching. He must see her; hearing her over the phone is no longer enough. He tries to catch sight of her face, a new wrinkle, a scar, her crooked smile, a tic, a sign, a clue, some trace of change, something tangible, something. . . .

Laziness, torpor of the multicolored anthill in the afternoon sun. Suddenly, a woman, tall and slim. Beautiful, elegant, oh yes, she must have been very beautiful, smooth forehead, clear eyes, her thick, shining hair pulled back in a bun. . . . There she is, she's coming, absolutely unhurried, an anonymous queen, shattered, jowls sagging, shoulders drooping, back bent, her smile crooked, humiliated, mean. Cream-colored suit, orange silk blouse. A large maroon leather bag on her left shoulder; in her right hand are two plastic bags full—of bombs, lettuce? Actress, terrorist, a countess rehabilitated through work, a housewife, a clerk, a nanny. Out of breath, distracted, wearily dragging her bags. Exhaustion, wrinkles, venom. Those lines, patience, habit, ancient conditioning rewarded daily . . . oh, and still, no . . . it's too much, she can't anymore.

Her eyes blank, she stops by the pillar and puts her bags down. A fat gray rat slips out through a basement window. Some young show-offs leave the line and start chasing the rat. Run down, surrounded, the animal, its tiny, lively eyes darting, tries to escape. The boys have cornered it, the animal emits shrill squeaks, they roar and roar with laughter as they kick it around, a bleeding ball. The lady fiddles with her hair, lowers her eyes, hangs her head so she doesn't have to see. She wipes her forehead with a handkerchief, tries to regain her composure, grabs her bags, leaves. She passes by the entrance to the apartment building, the pharmacy, the tobacconist, here she is at the hair salon, she keeps on going, slowly, face tight, elsewhere.

"Try your luck!" . . . She is startled, turns, sees the funny little man, smiles. Daydreams, fantasies, horizons. A step to one side, a step back. "Try your luck!" the clown selling lottery tickets keeps repeating. A waft of fresh air, sugar candies, prairies. The buffoon annihilates age, hierarchy, quotas, his voice insists, trills, calls, promises, the tempter knows all the tricks—the slightest hesitation, regret, nostalgia, wham!—you're in the trap. "Try your luck, try your luck, ladies and gentlemen," the liar proclaims unremittingly, humbly.

The woman is still smiling, surprised. She opens her handbag, rummages among her little notebooks, handkerchiefs, ball-point pens, pillboxes, but where's her wallet? "Try your luck, try your luck!" . . . But I am here, me, in the heart of the heart of all, coiled, invisible, cloven-footed, a paltry, skeptical, mediocre demon. I only know what is sure, true: the dice are loaded, *señora*, in this penny lottery you'll win nothing, nothing but sorrow.

Her right hand rummages furiously, her left still holding the bags of groceries and bombs. "Try your luck, try your luck . . ." But I am still there, watching, hidden in my hole, protective, an invisible bomb: a crap lottery, *señora*, a sham, just wind, *señora*. But in vain! . . . She won't hear it, she won't give up, she wants to take the chance. She still wants, she wants, she wants to want, she . . . On her face that serene look of bygone happiness. She searches, rifles. Her hands are white and coarse.

His eyelids suddenly shut out the explosion of the afternoon sun.

SEASCAPE
WITH BIRDS

THE STAGGERING, exhausted bodies should have been brought here, to the deserted edge of the sea, and stretched out on the cold moist autumn sand so that they could hear once more the muffled gurgle of the approaching liquid horizon. The greenish, soothing foam would have washed away all their humiliation; they would have joyfully let themselves be covered by the waves like large, wet veils.

Or, on a summer day, on a forced march, the herds forbidden to raise their eyes, sharp-edged stones burning under their feet, the scorching flour of the sand, flattened to the ground at the crack of a whip or a pistol shot, hundreds of yellow bodies, burning, transparent; lunar traces of chalk. They would have closed their eyes to die in sweet sunny reconciliation, like rows of skeletons, submitting, licked by the sea's heavy tongues, slowly being assumed into the sky.

If only the trains carrying them reached here, the few survivors could have descended the high, dusty cliff to the jagged shore. It would have been better had they been forced to watch, for hours on end, the fluid violet horizon, the silky tremor of spring. Transfixed for days, weeks, an entire year, before the

201

same scenery. Had they experienced this feeling of pointlessness, endlessness, they might not have chased after time so greedily, they might not have burst, like children dazzled by pretty words and colored beads, into the fevered confusion of the streets. In the sorrow of the moment, some, perhaps, might have felt the happiness of solitude.

The boy, the boy at least, would have deserved the cold, moist winds, the blaze of mirrors, summer. He should have been brought here long ago, thought the man overcome by indolence and sleep. For years on end I would have known only the light and the happy sobs of the water, I could have understood why nature means nothing to me, why even this all-encompassing roar has become—I would never have believed it—for me so . . . But he fell back heavily into the soft wave of the pillow and was unable to rise again.

He lost himself happily in the depths until the woman's cold, slender fingers found him again. Cool ripples of water fluttered against his neck, the hot ridge of his ear. He awoke startled, confused, in the past. He remembers that he had once come here with a girl, long ago. The explosion of reckless bodies. He would have let himself be devoured, whenever, by anyone. At the time the girl had felt it, the wildness in him. She had become tense, hostile. Her lissome young body became a long piece of steel that bent under the weight of her suffering until, in their violent embrace, it burst in a rain of silvery sparks. Their youth: a bloody membrane; the glasslike breaks, the reconciliations; the torture of frail, melancholy cannibals; hypocrisy, cruelty; the great feral leap. But his face was lost in the past; the hurried despot of a weak flame that was hungry for every wind.

In the morning he would have found her at the window or running on the deserted shore. Or asleep, drowsing until noon. Or suddenly released, in a flood of tears and kisses, from a nightmare in the too long night that had separated them. At the end of any day, any night, she would shatter, in a fraction of a second, the balance they had won after so much hardship. He was tired, unprepared, even then, for these reverses. The surprises would in time have become ever more exhausting, unbearable. He had not held out; for a long time he had no more than . . . Reeling, rising to the surface.

Through the haze of sleep he made out the green window frame, the woman's long, plump legs, her delicate white hands. Gradually he recognized her. So he is no longer young, then, no longer the keeper of that wild phantom. The days had entered into a calm accord. He found himself out of strength but at peace with the others and with himself, a child surrendering in her arms like gentle waves, in the warmth of the large, adult woman who mothered his days and nights but not the ever-growing void between two thoughts.

The cold of the bed's metal bar was pressing deeply into his thigh. The pain woke him, but his movements were slow and sleepy. Weakly, he tried to pull up his thin trousers of faded blue denim. Without getting out of bed he slowly and painfully raised one leg and then the other. His trousers caught at mid-thigh, and instead of pulling them up to his waist he let them hang, stupidly, below his belly. He had reached for his undershirt and was lifting it slowly, sluggishly, over his head.

"You know very well that all this means nothing to me," he mumbled. The woman was caressing his hair and—he could feel it without looking at her—smiling. His lost, childlike air touched her.

He raised his foot in the air; the wind cooled it. Then he pressed it to the tiles, his leg against the metallic edge of the bed. The coolness always calmed him. In the autumn he loved squalls, wind, water above him, a blanket of redemption.

"Why do you always swim with your head underwater?" she

asked him. Or he thought she had. He took his time answering, as if he had not heard, or because he could not get his head through the undershirt. "Why with your head?" the woman wanted to know, irritated or joking. Perhaps that was all she had asked, probably because of the way he was putting on his undershirt, lazily, like a sleepy child rushing to get to school. It is here, to the edge of this crashing sea, that the boy should have been brought long ago. To feel this thick verdigris bitterness obscuring the horizon, gathering from the deep, invading the whole October sky; or the sea's smooth plains in summer, gilded, vaguely inkstained, the swimmers lost in the distance, far from the bustle of the fevered beach; or in winter the white ash of the swells, the icy, desolate crags covered in snow.

As a boy he would have learned to swim, free and alone, to die in an excess of pleasure, not fighting the water, at peace, powerless, his eyes, his mouth, his nostrils filled with the flowing water. Free from himself, from the others, borne toward silence on pillows of water he would be no one's, everyone's.

"It's cold, keep it on," the woman whispered. They were leaving the yard; she covered his shoulders with a thick cloth shirt, and she was holding him up, since he was buckling at every step.

The rough, spiny grasses, the clumps of weeds in the ruts, the dry, dusty earth, the fatigue of this dawn, and the glassy reflection, bloody purple, of the horizon: they all slowed the climb. The man let himself be gently pulled by the arm around his neck. He could feel her fresh, pleasant skin, like that of a young mother, serene, magnificent.

Almost noon in the torrid heart of summer: the bus had stopped in front of the hotel; you could not see the beach from there. A young man had arrived, at last, to find his own ground. ... Long, confused years, adolescent fervor, the emptiness and the bustle of the lecture halls, the fever of books and debates, puberty stupidly dragged out in poverty, blindness, and dreams, until at last he could have the pounding of the sea, the explosion of his limits, the bursting of the sun over the whole horizon. It was as if the sky were dancing; red, orange, yellow parasols on the silvery crests of the waves. Fine blue streaks of light surging from all sides; the tumult, so long awaited, of the ultimate embrace. He had fainted, perhaps, upon finding his landscape, understanding why the mountains, lakes, hills, the glorious dusks of the steppe, before which he had lived, exiled, among so many others, had not overwhelmed him, not like this . . . then, every year, every season, profound rediscoveries and his collapse into them: balance in the heart of disorder.

The mornings reclaimed him from the nights with increasing difficulty. Torn, like now, from the mellow torpor of sleep, he was a cold, wet rag fluttering helplessly in the chill of dawn. From time to time he heard, beside him, the woman's lucid, sensual voice, clear and full. The joyous vigor, the quiet tenderness, the camaraderie with which she protected him surely deserved more than his reluctant answers.

Seeing the sun rise over the sea and all that, it's not what I . . . he was starting to say again. His elbow had bumped her firm, round breast, and he leaned up, groggy with sleep and sleeplessness. It doesn't mean anything, he would have mumbled, not even if I had come here in time, as a child, just back from over there, or as an adolescent, if the walls in me had tumbled when they should have, when there still was time, sparing me all these delays, had they come more quickly and lasted longer, those seasons when I returned here as a young man, the keeper of that rebellious, feline soul. . . . The cold and damp were chilling him. He would have loved to shrink himself into words if he could. Into a single word, and so to surrender himself to the woman.

Nature never spoke to me, I never saw it. I felt it, rarely, on my skin and in my nostrils. And now I no longer recognize my place; discovered so late, it rejects me. It's been two autumns since it abandoned me . . . he would have wanted to tell her, the woman deserved to know how he was losing touch with what had seemed to be his inner being, how much he was scared by this rupture. Like a frail child in danger, he picked up obscure signals from which he had to hide. Only her large, generous breast could still protect me, the rest no longer . . . but he was shivering, stiff from cold and exhaustion.

His arms, head, and shoulders hung heavily. His feet pressed down on the moist earth and rose sluggishly for the following step. His eyelids twitched slightly, narrow slits in the bluish fog that was thinning all around him. Morning had accepted him after all, he could feel it, even if the blow of this brutal awakening and the protracted effort of the climb exhausted him. He would have liked to confess to her, at last, his weariness, his anxiety. The woman pushed him on gently, supporting him so that he would not fall.

They had reached the crest of the hill. They were descending the steep slope to the coast, slipping on the wet grass. Arm in arm, they steadied themselves with their free hands. After having walked so far and climbed the ridges leading to the cottage at the cliff edge, they were looking for shelter. The wind was blowing hard.

He was infuriated, of course, by the determination of the vacationers, clustered together somewhere in the vicinity like a prayer group, not to miss the sunrise, and by the bright enthusiasm with which the woman agreed to their plans. Her approach maintained, however, a tender complicity, he had to admit, as if she were administering some subtle therapy. Methodical, patient, careful not to attack his biases, his objections, opening him up slowly to some new, unwished-for little pleasure that he could never have cared less for but that, astonished and soothed, he eventually accepted.

And so she brought him all the way up here, aware of the hatred that was growing inside him for her and for everyone because of these ridiculous outings. She was careful, though, to choose a spot away from the others, to spare him their presence. The cold, too: she had taken care to lead him to one of the deep hollows, like bomb craters, in the precipitous slope. She seemed to know the area well. She watched him carefully the entire way: frozen, wretched, furious. Everything would calm down, she was convinced, in the shelter from which they would watch the sun rise toward them out of the sea.

"Sit down, you too," insisted the woman, sensing that his indifference was giving way to hostility. She was waiting for the man to give up, depressed, all resistance. Right now he was looking disgustedly at the wet clumps of grass, the shell-shaped seat dug out of the clayey wall. He wanted nothing. She was familiar with his slow steps to compromise, when his revolts could flare up unexpectedly with a final, aggravated violence. His silence, his protracted apathy would have worried her had she not been able to cope with his surprises in her usual spirit of calm but firm competence.

Dawn had already broken, greenish and transparent; the dull downy clouds lifted, uncovering the ample bosom of the horizon breathing among the swells. On the wave crests, a flock of gulls rested, bobbing up and down like an obedient brood of ducklings. Clusters of them rising and falling in the same slow rhythm.

"Look over there, in the distance, to the left. A little more to the left, next to the dark line," the woman said, pointing out the direction. Her voice sounded even clearer. Fresh, deep.

Indeed, two symmetrical splashes of water appeared intermittently out at sea, bursting up violently, spraying water far and wide.

"It's Andrei and Ema. They're doing the butterfly." Without a doubt it was they, those slim, sturdy twins, the children of his

brother-in-law, the painter. Out of shyness, they were too boisterous. Guilty, ill at ease among others, itching to leave, falling
silent, embarrassed, moving away clumsily, stiffly. All of a sudden serious and grave. He had often watched them. It was true,
from sunrise on—before sunrise, so people said—brother and
sister were inseparable. They would go off together, diving into
the pristine black waters of the night, opening the gates of a
new day. Even on a day like this, when the entire group, up
early to catch the dawn, wanted to find them and include them
in the ridiculous collective outing. Up still earlier this time,
much earlier than the others, they were already far away, out
at sea, strange sovereigns of the empty expanse; no one could
reach them now, no one could disturb them.

I've never been able to master water like that. Nor swim, not
enough. Only short distances, as long as I can touch bottom. A
sort of cheating, or rather the pleasure of allowing myself to be
taken over, to disintegrate. Water above, all around, I've never
wanted anything more, my head under water, losing conscious-
ness. A voluptuous and cowardly drowning, since I have never
had the courage to give in, as I want to, the courage to let
myself drown, be carried away, delivered, a viscous flowing, a
decomposition, in fact. . . . The man slid his hands under his
thighs.

He had already felt the thick dampness on his elbows and
shoulders. Rotted weeds—or rather something else, blood. He
raised his elbows to look at them. He felt under his legs. Same
thing: the denim moist, sticky. An oozing liquid filled his palms.
He was overcome by a wave of disgust. Tense, the woman
watched every change in him.

He could feel that his trousers had become wet to the waist.
But it was not the cold moisture of the earth. Rather a sort of
warm, thick sap. He didn't look, he didn't want to.

A scream, the woman uttered a short scream, horrified at the sight of his red hands. Then he looked, too, bewildered, at his bloody fingers. He could not have sat on a piece of broken glass or a sharp bit of metal. He would have felt the cut, the blood. The spot was instead soft, pleasant. He looked at his hands again, aghast. His eyes had become large and troubled; his lips twitched in horror and disgust.

. . . *The hawk had been chasing the bird for a long time, in the thickness of a moonbeam, through the silent emptiness of the night that was swallowing us in its yawning sky. A sea in which we floated with no pain other than the dream of this lone bird, its flight reflected in the indifferent oily sheen of the water. It climbed higher and higher, longing to freeze in the ether, to die before being seized by destiny, and so be spared the coupling to come, furious, voracious. The savage flapping was coming closer and closer, as though to protect the bird for one instant more from the frigid heights, to take it still warm. The bird had wheeled around several times, more and more vulnerable, lost, prolonging the joy of its ultimate flight. The air became heavier but the bird flew calmly, effortlessly; waiting for the attack, resigned, ready to fill those jaws hungering for blood and heat. The hawk struck as the bird's last strength was ebbing away. . . . We, I remember, we leaped back, frightened; our arms suddenly struck the iron edge of the bed. We tossed uneasily in our sleep when the hawk, its prey dripping blood, began to dive over us into the ravine of this nightmare, where it would have devoured its victim, but the prey disgusted it, being too alive, yet helpless, much smaller than it had seemed from a distance, a burning arrow of blood. The abandoned carcass of a bird suffocated beneath my heavy, warm body dragged out here to wait for the sunrise.*

He had risen, silent, white-faced, bent with the terror and exhaustion of a morning that had rejected him.

He was holding his bloody hands up to his shoulders, like a prisoner. She followed him with her eyes, helpless, looking first at his drawn face, which now seemed waxen, then at his blood-stained trousers.

A step, he had climbed one step down the slope. As though

he wanted to go toward the sea. To cast himself into the deep, ever deeper, purged, healed of the last traces of this wound. As if he still felt the bird near him, inside him. To surrender himself to the water rather than to the woman with whom he had long known himself to be bound forever.

He took another step and looked again at his hands. In the distance, through his parted fingers, he saw the gulls sleeping on the swells. They had become red stains, as had the shimmering surface of the sea, which was coming, calm and vast, to meet him.

The sun had risen just over the twins, who were frenetically thrashing in the calm waters. Even the sand seemed to have turned red. The sun had covered the horizon, the sea coming alive, surging, a redemption, as he had wished it to be. To enter into the sunlight, under the thick liquid expanse that keeps drawing you in, swallowing you, into the deepening sky. A last, weaker, but total immersion. The sea flows more and more slowly, calmly, freely, a tender annihilation. The chance to be caught, still alive, to accept the embrace of death.

The twins had long since disappeared into the too bright light; he had forgotten them. The woman caught up with him at the water's edge. Her warm shoulder brushed him; he felt her cool, refreshing fingers in his hair and on his neck.

"It was a gooseberry bush. Red gooseberries. You sat right on top of them. Don't be afraid. It was only a few crushed gooseberries," she murmured, sisterly, anxious, trying to keep up with him. Her voice sounded deep and troubled; her mouth was fresh, hungry.

OCTOBER,
EIGHT O'CLOCK

ONE A step ahead of the other, they pass the narrow stalls. The woman in front, with a resolute gait. The man to her left, moving slowly.

A rhythmic flash of the knee: her red cape parts agitatedly with each step of her long leg. Her heel strikes the pavement, electrifying her body, which shudders, struck and wounded each time by the shock and the sound, as if the violence of her nervous gait compensated for her extreme frailty.

The man keeps the same slow pace. Yet the distance between them remains the same, only a step, as if the alarm sounded by her had failed.

Pyramids of huge, polished bell peppers. Mountains of peppers and tomatoes; through the gaps, the heavy black sleeve of a peasant's arm. Suspect crates of apples, yellow as lemons. Purple plums falling onto a scale of zinc. A shawl bent over a bunch of carrots. White table, white aprons hovering over blocks of white cheese: moist, reddened fingers covered in a film of cheese. Fast-talking and shrewd merchants moving their large, knotted hands on the scales. Bulbous sponges of coral, excrescences of huge Martian brains: cauliflowers. Dusty sacks of potatoes next to rough peasant boots. A puffy white face above a circle of dull earth-colored pears. A muffled din under the green glass awnings. A greenish light on the yellow spherical pumpkin slices that grin with wet dentures of seeds.

Perhaps she had expected too much of the day before. The vain accumulation of the hours on the anniversary, the man's neutrality, his prolonged silence.

Only at night, late, had he turned suddenly toward her eyes, cold from the wait. His hesitant voice filled the room with uncertain words. Intermittently, fragments of sentences reached their target. Tired words—about friendship, fatigue, tenderness—until he saw her pale face, her lips moving to answer.

Surely she was contradicting him; her blue gaze had been aroused, misty, trembling, charged with emotion. She said that their bond, always vulnerable, and their painful affection would last. It was stable precisely because it was painful, definitive, no matter how unsettled it seemed. Her answer had masked, for a while perhaps, his guilty surrender.

They came closer—perhaps abandoning their stiffness, their excessive delays; their movements were no longer evasive, slow, heavy; their passion had revived. The impatience of another time made them feverish and they saw each other again as they once had been: on fire, tender.

He had then turned off the light, of course. But he turned it on again immediately; he could no longer bear the dense darkness. The emotion had made him vulnerable; his fear had returned. And he listened to her warm, trembling voice.

Like orphans, she was saying . . . a couple of strange orphans, lost in the empty world, wandering in the desert, clinging desperately to each other, finding protection only in this . . . each time one falls, the other picks up the load for a little while, regaining strength; and later they reverse the roles, like a couple of children trading boasts.

He turned off the light again, then turned it on; the words had linked their cold, tired arms, and morning found them awake, unraveled by tension and sleeplessness.

This chilly weekend drove them, at dawn, into the streets. Dazed on a still, deserted Sunday morning. They forged through the cold, foggy air and weak light, the noisy market-place: muffled murmurs, crackling nutshells lost in the bottoms of sacks, the sound of cabbage leaves ripped like starched shirts, thick pumpkin shells cleaved by the cold ax, rows of kerchiefs and caps like so many gingerbread men.

They leave the hubbub of the market, the woman one step ahead of the man, who wraps his black-, green-, and red-checked scarf over the collar of his sand-colored trench coat. They walk along the wet sidewalk, up the slope of the silent street.

She presses her hands against the cold wall. Slender white hands with long, pale fingernails. The two are standing at the corner of an empty, stone-quiet street. She shivers under the soft shoulders of her furry cape, her face floating in the frozen air that penetrates her high cheekbones, the hollow of her eyes, her throbbing temples. She no longer sees her companion; she is looking elsewhere, nowhere, or perhaps toward the abandoned swing in the rock-strewn square between the apartment buildings.

The transparent blue of her moist eyes, her hands pressed against the cold, dirty plaster of the wall, an arm's length away from his fallen, bristled face. The deep cloud, the blue lake of her eyes wounded by his opacity.

"I was a sick, lonely child. Without strength . . ." she says after a while, her voice fragile, broken; her breath lifts a small round cloud from her whitish lips.

The man, his back half turned to her, tries to ignore her beauty, enlivened by her anxiety, by a sharp, cutting brightness that reminds him of the delirium of a night he ought to forget.

The weight of the night constricts his thin, arid body. He would rather not listen; let the words dissolve the very moment they arise, or let them be repulsed by the impenetrable shield of his absent body, or immediately incorporated and dissolved, lost in the lazy body of his bitter, apathy-blessed middle age. He looks straight ahead at the stained wall of the building in front of the open space with the swing. He cannot find the strength to recall whether these words without remedy, which were better not repeated, were not in fact his own, torn from inside him by a voice that only seemed alien.

Before the gray, bloody wall inscribed with black finger-prints—rotten stains—opens the narrow space of the play-ground. Well-beaten ground, made uneven by the corners of carelessly laid stones, by little mounds of poor, dry grass. A rusty green . . . yes, her long dry hair at dawn sometimes takes on the tint of verdigris.

A reddish board: one end down, the other up. The center is connected to a cylindrical log on which the seesaw rises, de-scends, swings up, down, and up and down again, swoosh, swoosh . . . a humble shelter among the surrounding apartment buildings. Next to it the metal frame of an unused swing, improvised with thick pipes driven like poles into the ground. Two unmatched seats hanging on chains from the crossbar: one rather wide, the other short and narrow, child-sized.

The girl approaches the swing hesitantly. A country girl, about sixteen. The darks of her eyes alive to the joy of the morning. A cloudless brow under the black kerchief. She puts down her double pouch: two camel humps next to the cracked valise. She straightens her back, one hand resting on her waist. A dress with yellow flowers over a pair of blue pants. Moist, pink lips slightly swelled with fatigue. The black arch of her long, tousled eyebrows. She stands next to the bigger seat. She puts the belt around her and fastens the hook, her thick, bluish hands holding the rusted chain.

"If it didn't seem absurd, if words didn't make everything

seem incredible, a trick . . . Believe me, with the passing of the years I have become younger. Only now do I truly understand the force of what has happened, the weight, the tension of the days. I accept laughter; it doesn't scare me the way it used to. Nor do pleasures, nor the harshness of the game, nor the load of the words, nor the doubt. As if driven constantly from a sort of magic void . . ."

The girl in the swing waits, unmoving, looking up to the top of the walls rising around her, upon which rests a small rectangle of gray sky. She discovers the couple leaning against the corner of the building before her. Without blinking, she meets the gaze of the man, who has been watching her for some time.

Still exposed to his intense gaze, she is curious but calm, grateful for the rest and the fresh air. His windblown head is down there somewhere; she sees him again for a fraction of a second, then another, when the seat touches the ground; it's only a moment, then the girl is higher up again; she drops down, and goes once more flying far above those two figures, stonelike on the frozen soil.

"Only now do I feel I have gathered some strength. It's possible that I may just be able to manage now. . . ." *

The words fly by, light. The pleasure of flight multiplies them, garlands of air, ever widening festoons, clouds of invisible swarming insects, rich bliss, tension, poison, bitterness, and freewheeling nostalgia, continuous attacks until the great void is saturated, until the darkened atmosphere thickens, leavened, suffocated by overflowing trifles, continuously breaking down layer upon compact layer . . . but the man turns around, awaits her moist blue look, places his cold hand over her long dry fingers with their smooth, pale fingernails. The woman smiles at him.

"So many years together already. Yesterday, our anniversary . . . incredible. How fast. . . . The possibility, the gift . . . vital energy, the pleasure and the strength to live. Life's energy, I mean . . . may we recapture it. Like two orphans clutching each other against fear and emptiness."

He turns her around gently, to the screech of the lever against which the pendulum rubs, up, down, up down; *the girl's deep dark eyes rise, descend, happy, full of the energy of the new day; and again, the legs in the jogging pants dance with the rising and descending seat.*

"Happiness should come my way now. I think that only now do I have the strength to live it. Perhaps suffering, too."

They are silent, they watch her: *she swings, lost in thought, without a care.* The man's chin trembles from the cold, his lips tighten; it's ridiculous for him to isolate himself so; he feels his guilty indolence; his fingers intertwine with the woman's; she responds, eagerly, with a fleeting squeeze.

Reconciliation: a gray wall with greenish stains. A slow see-sawing, forward, back, and again. The swing, the girl, the morning cold, the screeching chains, up, down, up, the glassy, frozen sky. A full upward sweep, then once more the rhythm evens, slows.

Her hair of rusted gold flutters above the red cape. No one would interrupt the pulsating of the stars, the infinite motion, the sad, quiet heart of truth. A blue tear in which the creaking swing dangles patiently: an illegible, opaque sky: the man's fingers keep squeezing, until suffering no longer fills the long, thin hands: the woman does not read his frightened expression, which becomes harder and more intense. Behind them, more and more footfalls, shuffling, voices. The street awakens, impatient and hostile. The silence holds sway a moment longer, untouched.

ABOUT
THE AUTHOR

Born in 1936, in Bukovina, Romania, Norman Manea was deported at the age of five to the Ukrainian internment camp of Transnistria. His fiction, which is preoccupied with the trauma of the Holocaust and with daily life in a totalitarian state, has been translated into more than ten languages. He is now a professor of literature at Bard College.